"We Need To Talk."

Such arrogance. She used to find it attractive. Oh, who was she kidding, she still did. There was something about a man who knew what he wanted and made no bones about it.

"Yes, we do," Ava said, trying to project a little arrogance of her own.

Christos arched an eyebrow at her. He said nothing more, and the silence built around them. Ava brushed her hands down the sides of her skirt and told herself she wasn't still the small-town girl he'd once seduced. But she felt like she was.

She tried to figure out what to say, but all the words running around in her head sounded banal. Best to be blunt.

"So…why are you here?"

"To claim your son, the Theakis heir."

Dear Reader,

The Greek Tycoon's Secret Heir was inspired by two things.
The first was my cousin Patty Ann's descriptions of Greece
when she visited there just after college. Her stories were
lush and vivid. I think I fell in love with the country at that
very moment. Years later I still haven't visited, but in my
imagination I've been there many times. And I always have
a strong, handsome Greek man at my side…well, that's the
fantasy, isn't it?

The second thing to inspire me was actually my hero,
Christos. I was thinking about how our life sometimes
changes unexpectedly, and we find ourselves thrust into a
role that we had never anticipated. In Christos's case, he
was the second son of a powerful man. The spare, not the
heir, and he partied hard, did whatever felt good and in
general lived only for himself. To become the man he was
meant to be, I knew that he was going to have to face a
challenge. For Christos, the change comes when his brother
is killed in a plane crash. Suddenly, Christos isn't the
second son anymore…he's the only son.

Ava Monroe is a woman who once defined herself with
lies. She grew up poor and was embarrassed by that
poverty, so she created a fantasy background for herself.
When she met Christos, she wasn't mature enough to
realize that lies have a way of coming back to haunt you.
Five years later she is much more mature, when Christos
comes back into her life.

Please enjoy this story and look for *The Wealthy
Frenchman's Proposition* next month from Silhouette
Desire.

Happy reading!

Katherine Garbera

KATHERINE GARBERA

THE GREEK TYCOON'S SECRET HEIR

Published by Silhouette Books

America's Publisher of Contemporary Romance

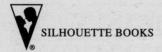 SILHOUETTE BOOKS

ISBN-13: 978-0-373-76845-5
ISBN-10:   0-373-76845-1

THE GREEK TYCOON'S SECRET HEIR

Recent books by Katherine Garbera

Silhouette Desire

†*His Wedding-Night Wager* #1708
†*Her High-Stakes Affair* #1714
†*Their Million-Dollar Night* #1720
The Once-a-Mistress Wife #1749
***Make-Believe Mistress* #1798
***Six-Month Mistress* #1802
***High-Society Mistress* #1808
**The Greek Tycoon's Secret Heir* #1845

†What Happens in Vegas…
**The Mistresses
*Sons of Privilege

KATHERINE GARBERA

is a strong believer in happily ever after. She's written more than thirty-five books and has been nominated for *Romantic Times BOOKreviews* career achievement awards in Series Fantasy and Series Adventure. Her books have appeared on the Waldenbooks/Borders bestseller list for series romance and on the *USA TODAY* extended bestseller list. Visit Katherine on the Web at www.katherinegarbera.com.

This book is dedicated to Patty Ann Souder
and her men Bill, Neil and Ian. Thank you, Patty,
for being the big sister I never had.

Acknowledgments

Special thanks to Aleka Nakis who helped me with
my Greek words. Any mistakes are my own.

One

"There's a man waiting for you in the principal's office," Laurette Jones said as she came into Ava Monroe's classroom. "I'll take care of your class until you come back."

"Is everything okay with Theo?" Ava asked. Her son was enrolled in pre-kindergarten at the exclusive Florida boarding school where she taught second grade. It was rare for her to be called away from her class in the middle of the day. The relative quiet of the warm February afternoon suddenly seemed ominous.

"I don't know. Karin asked me to come and get you." Laurette worked for principal Karin Andrews in the administration offices.

"Thanks, Laurette," Ava said, hurrying down the hallway, fighting the urge to run. She knew she was borrowing trouble, but Theo had asthma and they'd yet to find any medicine to get it under control. Just the thought that he might be having a breathing episode made her palms sweat.

She stopped by the nurse's office on her way and learned that Theo wasn't there. Relief swamped her. She hoped that Theo hadn't gotten into trouble in class. He wasn't a hellion but he was lively, and his teacher was pretty understanding most days.

She rounded the corner leading to the administration offices and heard a deep voice speaking in a heavy accent. She froze in her tracks. She'd never forgotten that voice, because she still heard it in her dreams. Christos Theakis. Her heart beat faster as she tried to tell herself she was imagining things. But she knew she wasn't. She rapped on the frame of the open door that led to Karin Andrews's office.

"Come in, Ava, we've been waiting for you."

She stepped into the office. And there he was. Christos leaned against Karin's desk, but straightened to his full height when she entered. He was about six feet tall and dressed in that cool European style that was both casual and sophisticated.

She brushed her hands down the sides of her floral-print skirt and told herself she wasn't still the small-town girl he'd once seduced. But she felt as though she was.

"Hello, Christos. I am so sorry about your recent loss."

He nodded his head solemnly at her offer of condolences. She saw grief and sorrow in his eyes, but he quickly controlled the emotions.

She'd had Christos and the entire Theakis family on the brain since they'd been in the news over the past month. His older brother, Stavros, sister-in-law, Nikki, and two nieces had been killed when their private jet had crashed minutes after take-off from Athens, Greece.

Ava, who had once been nanny to the girls, had burst into tears when the reporter had revealed the names. Things hadn't ended well with her employment with the Theakis family, but she'd adored those children.

Her son had been confused about why she was crying and had consoled her as only a four-year-old could, with his favorite stuffed animal, Monkeyman, and lots of hugs.

But the sting of knowing that the little girls she'd played with and cared for were deceased was still with her.

"We need to talk."

Christos's terse words snapped her back to the present. Such arrogance. She used to find it attractive. Ah, who was she kidding, she still did. There was something appealing about a man who knew what he wanted and made no bones about it. So different from the wishy-washy men in her circle, who struggled even to decide where they should eat dinner on a Friday night.

"Yes, we do," she said, trying to project a little arrogance of her own.

Christos arched an eyebrow at her and turned away. "May we use your office, Ms. Andrews?"

Karin flushed under Christos's gaze, something Ava had rarely seen the ultraprofessional woman do. She gave Christos a warm smile as she stood and walked toward the door. "Of course. And please, call me Karin."

The walnut-paneled door closed behind the principal with a distinctive thud. Christos said nothing and the silence built around them. Ava tried to figure out what to say but all the words running around in her head sounded banal.

Finally she glanced up at him and found he hadn't moved from his position against the desk. "So…why are you here?"

"To claim the Theakis heir."

Ava was exactly as he remembered her. The strawberry-blond hair, the delicate features and those wide blue eyes that were more mysterious than the deepest fathoms of the ocean. She had been unique to him. An anomaly in a world filled with people who wanted to be near him because of his money, his connections or his pedigree, she'd wanted to be with him in spite of all that. Or so he'd thought. She'd seemed fresh and innocent, and he knew that was a large part of the reason he'd been so attracted to her.

He would have bet his vast fortune that Ava was incapable of lying. And he knew now that he would have lost. He let the silence grow between them, watching her, knowing it made her uncomfortable. He still wanted her. Damn her for that. Even knowing she'd given birth to his brother's child…

Ava deserved the discomfort, he thought. She'd slept with him *and* his brother, and now he needed the child. His brother's son. God, what a mess.

Christos was the playboy of the family, the jetsetter who, for the most part, had always been more interested in his own pleasures than anything else. But for a few brief months during that summer when Ava had been in Greece…forget it, he wasn't going to rehash that.

He'd cast her out of his life, but everything had changed with Stavros's death. God, he missed his older brother and his nieces. He didn't miss his sister-in-law as much, but then Nikki had never been the kind of woman who'd wanted to be friends with him. He'd always been the second son to her. Not the heir.

His own temper was legendary, as was Stavros's, and the fight they'd had over Ava…well, it had taken on mythic proportions. And the part that stabbed him in the gut was that he'd thought they had years to work it out. Instead he'd never share a quiet moment with his brother again.

He knew what his father wanted from him. Take over the business, marry and produce more Greek babies. Ensure that the Theakis line continued. His father had sent him to Ava to claim the boy whom Stavros had paid her to keep quiet about.

He even knew what Stavros would say to him if he

had been able to see into the future…he would advise Christos to marry Ava and claim the boy as his own. Move them back to Greece where the boy could be raised to inherit the shipping empire that had been in their family for generations. His father's advice had been the same, but then Stavros and Ari were cut from the same cloth.

"I'm surprised you're here. I didn't think I'd ever see you again," Ava said at last.

He couldn't deal with the circumstances that had brought him here and he wouldn't talk about them with her. Not now. Tristan, one of his best friends, assured him that grief lessened over time, but Christos couldn't imagine this pain fading. "What does the boy know about his father?"

"The boy? His name is Theo. And I…I told him that you were an important Greek businessman whose interests kept him busy."

That he *was an important Greek businessman.* God, he couldn't believe she was still clinging to the lie that he was the father. He'd been careful every time they'd come together. Only slipping up once, he thought. But even then he'd pulled out as soon as he realized what he'd done. And Stavros…well, his brother had always been blunt when it came to sex and condoms—he didn't use them.

"A lie."

"You are a businessman. And you're always busy, at least, according to *Hello!* magazine. I don't see how

Stavros's death changes anything. You made your choice a long time ago."

He shrugged that aside. He wasn't going to get into the paternity issue again. That boy was a Theakis and he was returning to his family. They had the legal document she'd signed when she'd taken the money Stavros had offered.

He tried not to think about those long-ago days in Greece. As soon as he'd seen her with his brother he'd left, returning to a life of endless traveling and parties that he used to blur memories of their time together. He'd gone back to his old lifestyle with a vengeance. Being the second son meant his life was full of frivolity and socializing. No one expected anything of the second son. He had focused on his business interests during the day, but he'd partied all night.

"Where's the boy?" he asked.

Ava tucked a strand of hair behind her ear, eyeing him warily. Crossing her arms over her chest, she glanced out the window. "What do you mean, the heir? You told me…" Her voice quivered.

"I know what I told you but times have changed. I need you to be the woman I once thought you were."

That was nothing less than the truth. He needed something from Ava that even she couldn't have predicted. He needed her to be the kind of mother his had been. The kind of mother who could raise a boy to handle a world of privilege and expectation—because he wouldn't have enough time to do that.

"What woman was that?"

"One I could trust. My father's health is failing and he misses his grandchildren."

"Theo is nothing like the girls. He can't replace them," she warned.

"What do you mean?"

"He's American, Christos. He knows a little of your background and heritage, but he's not Greek."

"I'll teach him what he needs to know."

Still she shook her head. "Ari hates me."

"My father will love your son."

"I don't know. I'm not the naive young girl I was," she said.

"You're still young," he said. She was twelve years younger than he was, which he'd once thought excused some of the lies she'd told him. But he wouldn't be as forgiving this time.

"Being a mother has matured me in a way nothing else could have."

"Then you know that keeping your son from the Theakis family is not something that I can allow to continue."

She nodded. "When I saw the news about Stavros and his family, I thought about contacting you."

"Why didn't you?"

"I was afraid to deal with you."

"I can understand that," he said. He'd treated her almost cruelly when she'd come to him with the news of her pregnancy. But then, he hadn't been interested in cleaning up his brother's mess. So he'd turned her away.

After his father's heart attack, he'd hired a private investigator to find her. When the old man had seemed so fragile and Christos had made promises he wasn't exactly sure he could keep. Find the Theakis heir and bring him home.

He'd never forgotten Ava, despite the way things had ended between them. He'd come here to claim Theo as the Theakis heir, but watching the way the light played over her hair made him realize he wanted to claim the woman, too.

"I want to know the boy."

"Oh, okay. When?" she asked.

She was nervous; he read that easily in her stance and the way she was stammering to answer his questions. He told himself to lighten up—except, he couldn't. What he felt about her and the boy was too intense. She'd lied to him and he wanted to see her squirm a little now.

"Today, Ava. I think we can work this out on our own without involving my attorneys."

"Of course," she said. "I wasn't saying you couldn't see him. Just asking when you wanted to."

"Does he have our family name?"

"No."

"Was that in the agreement with Stavros?"

She crossed her arms under her breasts and arched one eyebrow at him. The show of temper made him hotter than he'd have thought it could.

"Why do you care? You said you wanted nothing to do with my child."

"But that has changed," he said. "Theo *is* a Theakis and I need him."

"As I just said, he shares *my* last name."

"That will be the first thing I change. I'll have my attorneys start the paperwork."

"Uh, isn't that moving fast? Why—"

"It isn't fast. Not after we've missed so much of his young life."

She flushed—with anger, he imagined—and nodded toward him. "I'm sure that Theo will be pleased to meet you. He knows your name."

"Very good."

She didn't respond to the last but he caught another glimpse of her temper in her eyes before she turned away.

"I'll have Karin call him out of class. He's a little afraid of the principal's office. Maybe you should wait in the gardens. I'll bring him to you."

Theo chattered as she walked him down the hall toward the gardens, asking her specific questions about Christos. But she really didn't know what to say. Finally they stepped out into the Florida sun and he slipped his little hand in hers, quieting as he looked at the tall man standing with his back toward them.

She knelt down next to her son and hugged him close. "He's very excited to meet you."

"Are you sure?"

"Yes, she is," Christos said, coming over to them. "Theo, I'm Christos Theakis."

Theo took Christos's hand and shook it. "Hello, Father."

Christos drew back and looked up at her sharply. She couldn't read his look.

"The Greek word for father is *baba*, Theo," Ava said.

Christos drew Theo into his arms and Ava turned away. It had been easy to believe that she was doing the right thing for her son by keeping him from Christos. Christos had been very angry during their last encounter, when he'd accused her of sleeping with both Theakis brothers. And she'd been unable to defend herself against that anger.

He'd wanted her to take a DNA test to prove paternity, but she'd refused, wanting him to trust her. She knew that she'd lied to him about other things, and had acknowledged those lies, but on this matter, she had needed him to believe her. Because, before the situation with his brother had blown up, he'd told her they'd moved past her falsehoods. And she'd needed that to be true for the relationship to survive.

She'd seen the proof that he'd moved on with his life in the pages of the tabloids and society magazines. But here in this quiet garden as he hugged Theo, she wondered if she'd made a mistake.

She edged away from them. Tried to remind herself of all the reasons she was no longer in love with Christos. Why she'd never really been in love with him in the first place. But, watching him, those reasons seemed flimsy. And her heart, which had been dormant during the five years they'd been apart, started beating again.

She was *so* not going there. Christos was the man who'd changed the entire course of her life, and she finally had it back on track. She wasn't getting involved with him again. Except—she'd have to, if he was going to act as Theo's father. She couldn't keep Theo from him now that he was reaching out to his son. The Theakis family was a close one, something her own wasn't, and she wanted that for Theo.

Karin stopped by to return Theo to class, leaving Ava alone with Christos. He stared after his son. Her throat tightened as she watched the cocktail of emotions rushing across his face. She'd always suspected there was more to Christos than the playboy image he presented to the world. She'd caught glimpses of the real man during the intense time they'd spent together. Enough to make her fall hard.

But this was only the second time she'd seen any overt evidence. The other time…well, that didn't bear thinking about right now.

"You've done a good job with him."

"Thanks. I…I'm not always sure what I'm doing. But he's a good kid."

"Yes, he is." Pushing his hands into his pockets, he walked closer to her.

"Why did you tell him I was his father?" Christos asked.

"You still don't believe me about that?"

He shook his head. "I gave you a chance to prove yourself to me, Ava. To prove that Theo is really my son, and you denied me."

"Because I wanted your trust."

"Once a liar."

"That's not fair, I apologized for those lies. I was young and thought you wouldn't want a girl from my background."

"Your very poor background," he said. "What better way to make sure you never had to go back to that trailer park than to bear the son of a Theakis."

She shook her head, trembling all the way to her soul from his words. "It wasn't like that."

"You can explain it to me another time. Right now you have two choices, Ava."

She still liked the way her name sounded on his tongue. Which really ticked her off, because she wanted to slug him for being a jerk about the past. She'd made mistakes, yes, but what was it about this stubborn Greek that wouldn't let him look beyond them? "What are they?"

"You can relinquish your rights to Theo and give him over to me to be raised as a Theakis."

"Why would I do that?" He had to be crazy if he thought she was going to give up her son.

"It is his right to be raised in our family. And you have had him to yourself for the last four years."

"You gave those years away," she said, and the past flashed through her mind. She knew the exact moment when she'd become pregnant. Remembered with clarity the way Christos's face had tightened with a mixture of lust and anger when she'd declined to stay in Greece and become his mistress.

He'd kissed her hard and soon anger had melted to lust and they'd made love in his study. The encounter hadn't been a sweet seduction; they'd both been so hungry for each other, knowing it was the last time they'd be in each other's arms.

She'd clung to his shoulders and he'd held her so tightly. He'd cradled her on his lap, and she'd realized that they'd forgotten to use protection. That he'd pulled out at the last moment.

He hadn't said anything and neither had she. Then a few days later everything had fallen apart with Nikki's accusations about her and Stavros. And Christos had sided with his sister-in-law.

"Maybe. But not anymore. I want Theo. I've taken over Theakis Shipping," he said, turning away from her and looking out over the lushly landscaped gardens of the school. "I'm becoming the heir I never had to be and I must look to future generations."

"Now you need an heir," she said. She was saddened to think that that was the only reason he was here. Not because he'd finally wanted to acknowledge he had a son and had been desperate to see him.

Oh, God, she couldn't let Christos hurt Theo. Wouldn't let Theo come to love a man who had ice in his veins. A man who could make love to a woman and hold her so close, as if he'd never let her go, then calmly accuse her of infidelity.

"The Theakis family needs Theo," he said.

This isn't about you, she reminded herself. But it was.

"You mentioned two choices."

"Yes, I did. If you are interested in remaining in your son's life, then I'm willing to marry you."

Two

The house he'd rented overlooking the Atlantic Ocean was large and lush but empty. Even with the staff of five he'd hired, it still felt so empty. Christos leaned deeper into the leather office chair, snagging the phone as it rang.

"How'd it go today?" Tristan Sabina asked.

Tristan was one of Christos's two best friends. The other was Guillermo de la Cruz. They'd formed an odd little triad of mischief makers and playboys for more than half their lives. They'd met at an exclusive boarding school in Switzerland and had bonded through their troublemaking antics.

The three of them had been tabloid fodder for longer

than he could remember, moving through life as if the world was their oyster. They'd started a business together in their twenties, a string of nightclubs located in posh hotspots all over the globe. The exclusive clubs, called Seconds, were the place to see and be seen the world over, and every night the bouncers turned away more celebrities, wannabes and hangers-on than they let in.

And Tristan, Gui and Christos were the kings of the kingdom they'd built.

Christos settled the phone between his ear and his shoulder and knocked back a shot of tequila. "Who knows? I thought she was going to hit me when I told her I was willing to marry her."

"You Greeks have no way with women," Tristan said. "You should have pulled her into your arms and kissed her senseless, then told her you were marrying her."

"It's not about her," Christos said, struggling not to get angry at his friend.

"It sounds as if it is," Gui said calmly, always the voice of reason, as he joined the three-way conference call. "You've never talked about what happened."

"Nor do I intend to."

"How was the boy?" Tristan asked.

"The boy was…he seemed…"

"What, Christos?" Gui asked. The three-way call was a little cumbersome, but it was the best way to keep in touch now that they all had other legitimate business concerns.

"He has Stavros's nose."

"You have the same one. It's the Theakis features. They bred true," Tristan said.

"Did you ask her again if Stavros was the father?" Guillermo asked.

"No. She lied before. Why wouldn't she again?"

Tristan cursed under his breath. "Do you want company in Florida?"

"No. I'm going to wrap up the legal arrangements for the boy and then fly back to Greece next week."

"What about the woman?" Guillermo asked.

"She's thinking it over."

"What exactly is she thinking over?"

"If she's going to marry me." Christos didn't want to think too much about Ava or his marriage offer. He could still remember the last time they'd discussed the subject, and hadn't that been a kick in the pants.

"Marriage? Is that the only solution?" Tristan asked.

"It is for me. I…"

"You still want her and you think that will keep it under control?" Gui asked.

"I'm not exactly thinking."

"True," Tristan said. "I'm scheduled back in Paris in three weeks, on the thirtieth. I can be at your place on Mykonos on the twenty-third."

An electronic beeping noise came through the line. "Me, too."

"You don't have to—"

"We know," Gui said. "I want to meet her for myself."

"Gui, she's not like—"

"I'm not saying she is. I just want a chance to see what kind of woman is the mother of the Theakis heir."

"So do I," Tristan said. "You and Stavros are so different."

"*Were* so different…hell, I guess we still are," Christos said.

Emptiness buzzed on the line. "Are you sure you don't need us?"

"Yes," he said, and tossed back another shot of tequila.

There was a rap on the library door. "I must go." He hung up the phone. "Enter."

"Sir, there is a Ms. Ava Monroe to see you." Antonio Montoyo was his butler and traveled with Christos wherever he went. Though Antonio was only fifteen years older than Christos, their relationship was closer to father and son than the one he shared with Ari Theakis.

"Is she alone, Antonio?"

"Ah, no. She brought along the boy, Theo."

And there was the rub. No matter what the truth was, the world was going to believe that Theo was his son. Nikki, his sister-in-law, had done too good a job of hiding all of Stavros's affairs.

"Send them back."

"Ah, sir?"

"Yes, Antonio?"

"You aren't dressed for receiving."

He arched one eyebrow. He'd just come in from swimming in the sea and was dressed in trunks and no shirt. Granted, it was winter in Florida, but the daytime temperature still wasn't cold. And he'd be damned if he'd change for Ava. He couldn't explain his feelings for her, hell, wouldn't even try, but she held a lot of cards with that small boy of hers and he wasn't going to give an inch otherwise.

"I'm fine. Better that she see me as I really am now."

"And that is, sir?"

"A playboy masquerading as the head of a Greek shipping line, a man of the sea like my father and brother."

"I've known you a long time, Christos, and you are nothing like either of those men."

"Enough," he said.

Antonio left the room with a small nod of his head. The butler's disapproval was something he'd deal with later. He respected Antonio. Despite Antonio's insistence on keeping up appearances, Christos knew he wouldn't fail to drop him some advice.

The doors opened a few seconds later and Ava stepped into the room. She'd changed. Dammit. She now wore a pair of faded old jeans that clung to the slim length of her legs and a cashmere sweater that matched the blue of her eyes. Her hair hung loose around her shoulders.

Theo stood next to her dressed in a pair of baggy navy sweat pants and a matching fleece top. They both thanked Antonio as the older man left.

"Have a seat," Christos said.

"Thank you for seeing us," Ava said.

"I was expecting you," he said. True, not this soon, but he'd figured she'd come to him with her answer.

"I know," she said, quietly.

She glanced at her son and then back up at him and he saw a hint of protectiveness in her gaze along with that other emotion he could never identify.

She cleared her throat. "I was discussing your proposal with Theo and he has a few questions."

He was surprised. But in a good way. Theo would one day run a multibillion dollar corporation. Learning to weigh options and make decisions was an important step to learn.

"What are your questions, Theo?"

"I want to know about Greece, *Baba*."

Baba. He hated hearing that from the little boy. He was Theo's uncle, not his father. He needed to talk to Ava and deal with this. But not in front of Theo. "Perfectly understandable. Come over here and I'll show you some pictures of our home."

The boy hesitated and Ava bent over to pick him up. "Ava, put him down."

She set him on his feet.

"Are you afraid of me?" he asked Theo.

The boy shrugged, his eyes the dark obsidian that Christos saw every morning in the mirror. He didn't want the boy to fear him. But, to be honest, he had no idea what to do.

He glanced at Ava and she straightened. "Come on, Theo. I'm curious about how the Theakis household has changed since I was last there."

They crossed the room together. And though he knew he held all the cards in this situation, he felt like an outsider.

"Does this mean that you've decided to accept my offer?" Christos asked.

"We've been talking it over. I want to make sure that Theo will be happy." Ava tried to keep her voice cordial. She'd spent the entire afternoon on the treadmill in her bedroom, running off the anger that had sprouted deep inside when he'd said he was *willing* to marry her.

She'd wanted to tell him to take a flying leap into the ocean and swim back to Greece, but Theo was enthralled by Christos. He'd spent all afternoon asking her questions about him. And then finally asked if he was going to have a father. And Ava's heart had broken. She did the best she could for her son, but she couldn't be a father.

Christos nodded at her in a way that revealed nothing of what he felt. Ava didn't know what she wanted from this meeting with Christos, but him sitting, aloof, behind that large walnut desk wasn't it.

He thought he held all the cards, she knew that. She could tell from the way he was staying seated in his position of power. She'd come to him. The problem was she was drawn to that arrogance. To the utter confidence that he exuded.

His chest was bare and she struggled to keep her gaze from it. From that gold medallion nestled in his chest hair.

He'd always been in good shape and he certainly hadn't let himself go in the five years since she'd seen him.

Too bad, because it would be so much easier to resist him if he'd developed a beer gut like many of her other male friends. Some sign of emotion from Christos would also make things easier on her but he was still the iceman when it came to feelings. The only time he'd ever revealed any fire had been when they'd made love. And, of course, when she'd seen the hard side of his temper.

Theo's hand trembled a little in hers. He wasn't afraid of Christos exactly, but his exposure to men had been limited. At the school most of the staff were women. Her best friend Laurette was engaged, but her fiancé, Paul, traveled a lot, so even he wasn't around much. Though he did make a fuss over Theo when he came to her house.

"The Theakis family compound is on an island in the Aegean," Ava said. They didn't just live on the island, they practically owned it. They had properties all over Europe and the world, but Mykonos was their base of operations.

Christos reached out and lifted Theo onto his lap. Her son looked so small against the thick muscles of Christos's chest and arms. He reached around Theo to hit a button on his computer and images started flashing up on the screen.

He leaned in low and for a moment brushed his nose over her son's head, inhaling deeply. Then Christos looked up at her and she saw a yearning in his eyes. But what did it mean? Did he want Theo, or wish that Theo was his son?

She regretted not taking the paternity test years ago, but a part of her still stood by her conviction. The man she'd made love to should have known she'd never lie about something as important as intimacy. The other lies she'd told…they were little ones.

She blinked back a few tears. She was looking for some sign that he wanted Theo for more than continuing his line.

Images from a past that she'd locked away flashed on the computer screen. Mykonos had changed little in five years. Why should it? The island dated back to the very beginning of recorded time and the few short years since she'd been there…

She realized she wasn't ready to take a trip down memory lane, not even to ease her son about his upcoming move to the Greek island. And she knew that Christos hadn't been kidding about taking Theo.

"Will you excuse me for a minute?" she said.

Both males looked up. "Where are you going?"

"I need to use the bathroom."

Christos nodded. "It's down the hall to the left."

She left the room as quickly as possible and stopped in the hallway. She heard the deep rumble of Christos's voice as he spoke to Theo, telling him about his heritage.

She realized that this situation was out of her control and she had absolutely no idea how to get it back. She'd dreamed of a time when Christos would return and claim Theo. Claim *her.* Yeah, that was the rub, wasn't it?

That she'd been waiting five years for him to realize he'd been wrong when he'd accused her of infidelity. And now he was here, offering her something she'd always wanted. The one thing she'd dreamed of when they'd first begun their affair. Yet she knew that saying yes to Christos's proposal wasn't going to make everything into that mythical happy ever after.

"Are you okay?"

She glanced up at Antonio. She wondered if he remembered her, or if the stream of women through Christos's life had made him forget.

"I'm fine, Antonio. I just needed a minute to myself."

"Of course. Why don't you go out to the gardens? I'll let Mr. Theakis know where you are."

"Thank you," she said, and followed Antonio's directions. She stepped out into the cool February evening. The smell of the ocean and the lush shrubbery surrounded her.

She followed a path to the center of the garden and found a bench that overlooked a small fountain of a triton—half man, half fish with a large, dragon-like tail. It was lit from the base and she watched the water spill out.

"Ava?"

"Over here," she called.

Christos came around the corner. He'd put on a fleece pullover and a pair of deck shoes. His hair was thick and black, rumpled as if he'd run his fingers through it.

"Where's Theo?"

"I sent him to the kitchen for something sweet."

Theo had a sweet tooth like nobody's business. Well, to be honest, that was one of the things they shared, so she limited any kind of junk food in their house. "Why?"

"We need to talk."

Christos sat down on the bench next to her. His body heat reached her in waves and she fought the urge to scoot closer to him.

"What have you decided?"

She shrugged, not ready to tell him yet. Not really sure if she was going to say yes to him and change her life for this man. At one time she'd been ready, but she wasn't sure she could risk her heart again.

Theo was smart and funny and concerned about what moving would do to his mother. In a candid moment he'd revealed that Ava's family had cut her off completely when she'd returned from Greece pregnant. Of course, the little boy hadn't put it in those exact terms, but Christos could read between the lines of Theo's simple words...*it's just Mommy and me.*

He hadn't wanted to personalize his relationship with Ava or her son too much yet, but it was too late for that. The little boy was slowly, shyly winding his way into Christos's cold heart, and Ava...hell she'd always been his Achilles' heel, hadn't she? He wanted her. Why the hell hadn't that changed?

Here in the moonlight she looked too fragile, too vulnerable to have done all the things he knew she had. And despite the fact that she'd played him for a fool, he had never wanted her to lose her family and their support.

What a damned mess this was.

"I have questions," she said, turning to face him.

Her eyes were big and wide, forthright and honest. He knew the honesty was mostly a mirage. But in this moment, with the soft trickle of the water in the fountain, surrounded by the lush scents of hibiscus and the fragrance of her perfume, it didn't feel like a mirage.

It felt too damn real. He hated that this woman made him vulnerable. With anyone else he would have swooped in, taken the boy and left. But not with Ava.

"About?" he asked her.

"When are you planning to leave?" she asked.

"Next week. I'm waiting for the paperwork—and your decision, of course. The lawyers think they can have the papers to officially make Theo the Theakis heir done on my timetable."

"I don't think I can leave next week. I can't leave the school in a bind."

"Does that mean you're coming with me?" he asked. The breeze stirred her hair and a strand blew across her face. She tucked it back behind her ear only to have it blow forward again.

He reached out and captured it, wrapping the strand around his finger. It was fine and soft like the sea mist when he was on his speed boat racing across the Aegean.

"Yes. I…I don't want Theo raised the way you were, Christos."

He liked the sound of his name on her lips. Always had. He dropped his hand from her hair and leaned forward, facing the fountain. The pounding of his heart and the racing of his blood through his veins made a mockery of his lauded self-control. How the hell could he still be so affected by her?

He stood up to give himself the position of power. She was just a girl, he thought, looking down at her. And he'd slept with many more sophisticated than she was. Why then was she the one he longed to hold again?

"How do you mean?" he asked. He'd had a great childhood, once he'd adjusted to living away from home. And it *had* been an adjustment, coming on the heels of his mother's death. But Tristan and Gui had been there from the beginning and he'd found a home away from home in their friendships.

"In boarding schools, away from home all the time. I know that's what the Theakis family does with their children."

Yes, she was intimately acquainted with how Stavros had raised his daughters, having been the Theakis nanny that summer long ago. He felt the quick burn of anger in his gut. "I won't discuss my brother with you."

"I wasn't talking about Stavros, but his daughters."

Remembered little-girl giggles made him turn away from her as tears burned his eyes. Little Vennie had always hugged him so tightly whenever she'd seen him. And Althea, ah, her kisses had been so sweet. God, he missed those two. Despite the feud with Stavros, he'd still seen his nieces once a month and they'd been close.

"I will of course consider your opinion in the matters of Theo's schooling, but the ultimate decision will be mine."

"Don't do this."

"Do what?"

"Be that arrogant Greek male."

"That's who I am. Get used to it."

She shook her head. "I can make it more difficult for you to leave."

"You are welcome to try. I'm sure that your *pro bono* lawyers will have some ideas as to how to help you, but they'll be playing out of their league. I've hired the best family law attorneys available here in the States. And I do have that agreement you signed for Stavros."

"What makes you think I can't afford a lawyer?" she asked.

"You're a teacher, living off your weekly paycheck," he said, stating the simple facts he'd read in the report his detectives had made.

"Stavros sent me some money when Theo was born," she said. "That was part of the agreement I signed."

"Are you going to use my brother's money to fight me on this issue?"

It made him feel like the worst sort of bully when she shrank back. Dammit, what was it about Ava that made him act like…an arrogant Greek male. He'd spent a good portion of his life trying to distance himself from that part, but she brought out his primal instincts.

"Maybe I will. I think there are a lot of benefits to Theo and I moving to Greece with you, but if you act like a jerk, I'm going to make it difficult for you."

"A *jerk*?"

"Yes, a jerk. You do know what that word means, don't you?"

"Yes, Ava, I'm familiar with it. I'm not sure why you are calling me one."

"You just asked if I'd use your brother's money to fight you. It's my money now, Christos. Mine and Theo's. I accepted it for his sake."

"Touché. I'll stop saying it's Stavros's. What else makes me a jerk?"

"Acting as if Theo is a commodity…calling him 'the Theakis heir.' He's a boy. I love my son. I don't want him to be banished to a sleep-away school," she said. There was a wealth of love in the way she spoke of Theo.

"Going to school will enable him to form bonds with future leaders. It's far more than just getting kids out of their parents' hair."

"He can do that in other ways. I want—"

"This isn't about your wants, Ava." She glared at him and he held back a smile. She tried to hide all of the fiery passion and temper underneath such a serene surface. But it was always there, waiting to break through.

"I'm afraid it is, Christos. This isn't going to be one of your dictates. I don't work for you or any of the

Theakis family anymore. And when it comes to Theo, I'm the final authority."

His gut instinct was to take the boy to the private airport where his jet was waiting and just leave. Once he was back on Mykonos with Theo, she'd have a difficult time seeing the boy again. He'd be charged with kidnapping the boy, but he paid his lawyers a lot of money and they'd figure a way to resolve that.

"You are not the *final authority* when it comes to Theo," he said.

"Yes, I am. There's no father listed on the birth certificate."

"Yes, but I have proof that Theo is a Theakis." He hated that piece of paper that he'd found in Stavros's private office four days after his brother's death. The legal document promised Ava an annuity in return for not making a claim of paternity against Stavros. The very money she'd just mentioned. But the paper did acknowledge that the baby was a Theakis.

"You may have that paper I signed, but that doesn't mean I'm going to just lie down for this," she said.

"I don't need threats. Just understand that Theo and I are leaving for Mykonos in less than ten days."

"I have one more question," she said.

He looked at her in the moonlight and tried to be objective. She wasn't *that* attractive. She was pretty, yes, but he couldn't explain the bone-deep desire he had for her. It went beyond looks. "Yes?"

"Why are you offering marriage?"

Three

It was tempting to just let Christos make all of the decisions and say he was forcing her into marriage, but she had to be strong for Theo. She wanted to be the kind of parent that hers never had been and that meant standing up for herself now.

"Marriage will legitimize Theo's birth," he said, his voice low and husky in the darkening light.

Whenever he spoke of Theo she felt as though she was missing something. "I didn't think there was still a stigma to that."

"Maybe here in America there isn't, but in my father's eyes there is. And with his legitimate heirs gone…"

Her heart broke at the thought of the deaths of Vennie

and Althea. And the fact that Theo would never know his cousins. But she also felt angry that Theo was an afterthought. "If that's all Theo is to you then I'm afraid we're done here."

"He's not only an heir."

She crossed her arms over her chest. "He's not?"

"What do you want from me?"

"I want to know what you really feel toward Theo."

"I like him. I see Stavros in him and I miss my brother."

She dropped her arms and felt her heart melt a little. She heard the truth in his words. "Okay, so all of that's why you want Theo. But why are you willing to marry me? I thought you could only marry a Greek woman."

A hard laugh escaped him. "Times have changed."

She walked toward him on the cobblestones stopping when only a breath separated them. She wanted...wanted to hear him say that he was offering marriage because he'd finally realized she was the one woman he couldn't live without. Looking into his obsidian eyes and seeing how guarded he was, she knew that was a fantasy.

"I'm not going to let you keep these barriers between us," she said, knowing she couldn't be the kind of wife that Nikki had been. Nikki had let Stavros push her to the background of his life, a place where Nikki was forced to watch her husband carouse with other women. Ava refused to blend quietly into the background as she might have five years ago when she hadn't been as sure of herself. Before she'd had Theo she might have compromised herself, but not now.

He took a deep breath, the warm exhalation brushing along her cheek. His hands fell on her hips and he drew her to him. "Then by all means come closer, my dear."

She brought her hands up, putting them on his chest to keep some space there. Why had she thought she could take control of the situation and Christos?

"This isn't what I meant," she said, but there was a rightness to his hands on her. She wanted to lean forward and put her head on his chest. To feel his arms around her once again. Oh, man, this had *bad idea* written all over it, but she didn't want to move away.

"This was always right between us," he said, the words uttered under his breath.

Yes, she thought. Yes, it was. She tipped her head back to meet his gaze. His lips were firm and full and so close to hers. She remembered the way he'd kissed her, and she sucked her lower lip between her teeth, biting down on it before she did something really stupid like lean forward and touch her lips to his.

Someone cleared his throat and Christos held her firmly against him when she would have jerked away.

"Yes, Antonio?"

"Master Theo is wheezing," Antonio said.

"He has asthma," Ava said, pulling away from Christos and running back toward the house. She had left her purse in the study and she hurried to find it. She grabbed her bag and found Antonio and Christos in the hallway. "Where is he?"

"Kitchen."

She ran down the hall in the direction that Antonio had pointed. She skidded to a halt, seeing her little boy sitting on the chair, his little chest going in and out as he struggled to breathe.

"Hey, baby," she said, sinking to her knees next to his chair.

"I'm fine," he said, the words breathy and not at all in his normal tone.

"No, you're not."

He shook his head. "Mama, I don't want to use the inhaler."

She didn't argue with him. She struggled with Theo and his asthma all the time. He hated the weakness and refused to acknowledge when he needed the medicine. "I know, baby."

She pulled out the inhaler and the long chamber that attached to it. She shook the inhaler. She was dimly aware of Christos standing quietly in the doorway, but she paid him no mind.

Theo glanced over his shoulder at Christos and then leaned into her shoulder. "I don't want *Baba* to see."

"It's okay," she said.

Theo shook his head.

She turned to ask Christos to leave but he'd come further into the room, leaning back against the table. "Mind your mother, Theo, we'll talk about this after you've had your treatment."

She lifted the inhaler toward Theo and he took it into

his mouth. She dispensed the medicine, counting quietly and watching him the entire time.

Christos put a hand on Theo's shoulder and when they were done, she looked up at him and saw a shadow of the same worry she felt for her son. It was a moment that brought them closer together after the nonsense on the patio.

Well, it hadn't been nonsense, she thought, but when faced with something like their sick child, it seemed silly. She wanted to marry him. It was all she'd ever wanted, so even though she wanted to know what had changed his mind about being her husband, she wasn't going to ask any more questions.

Theo needed the stability that having two parents would bring him. She saw the seeds of caring in Christos's eyes when he looked at Theo and she wanted that directed at her again.

She wanted to find a path back to the passionate couple they'd been that long-ago summer, and, without the outside influences of Stavros and Nikki Theakis, they might just have a chance.

"Tell me what's up, *paidi mou*?" Christos said.

Theo shrugged in that little-boy way of his. Ava put her arm around her son, struggling not to pull him tight against her chest because his breathing was easier now.

"I want you to like me," Theo said.

"Why wouldn't I?"

"Because I'm not perfect," Theo said.

"Yes, you are," Ava said.

"Your mother is right. To us you are perfect as you are. Don't try to hide something that's a part of you, especially if it can hurt you."

Theo nodded and Christos lifted the boy into his arms. Ava stood next to them, feeling the bond starting to form between father and son. She felt a rekindling of the love she'd always felt for Christos, only this time it was a little deeper than before.

Christos insisted on driving Ava and Theo back to their house, Antonio following with Ava's car. Antonio waited with Christos's vehicle, and Christos joined Ava as she settled the boy into bed. Their house was small, but very comfortable and welcoming. The living room was dominated by bookcases along one wall and a large chair that had a colorful blanket draped over the back of it and a large overstuffed pillow on it.

The walls were covered in pictures of Theo from birth until, if he wasn't mistaken, a few weeks ago. There were Christmases chronicled with visits to Santa.

He walked slowly down the hall looking at the pictures of the boy's life. He felt cheated by his own hand. Theo was his nephew; he should have stayed involved with him. He should have been there at the boy's christening, which was documented by photos and a certificate on the wall.

Of course, she'd had the boy baptized in the Roman Catholic Church instead of Greek Orthodox. His father would have a fit.

"Thanks for seeing us home," Ava said as she came into the hallway and partially closed the door to Theo's room.

"You're welcome. How bad is the asthma?"

"They don't know. He might outgrow it."

"I have it."

"What?"

"I know, shocking, isn't it? It runs in the family. My mother's side." His condition wasn't something he advertised and thanks to medication he kept it under control, but when he'd been a child it hadn't made his life easier. Hard to believe it now, but he'd been a pudgy, wheezing kid.

"Yes," she said. "I had no idea. You seem so fit."

"Fit?"

"You know what I mean."

"Strangely enough, I do. Swimming is good for the lungs. I'll show him some of the things I do to control it."

She nibbled on her lower lip, which brought to focus another reason he'd come back to her place. He wanted her. The arousal that had burned through him earlier in his gardens was back.

"Theo's afraid of water."

"What? The Theakis are of the sea."

She shrugged. Somehow she doubted that was going to make Theo realize that he should love water. "I don't know. I've tried to get him into the pool here, and in the ocean, and he won't do it."

"I'll take care of that," Christos said.

As they walked down her hall of memories, he felt

more the outsider than he had before. But that was nothing new. His entire life he'd been out of step with the rest of the world. Well, the world that his father had created.

"Do you have anything to drink?" he asked.

"Sure, come on in the kitchen," she said, leading the way into the bright room. There was a booster seat on one ladderback chair. He glanced around and saw the life she'd created for herself and Theo.

This was what he'd always imagined her life to be. This cozy, homey little place. And he knew he didn't fit in with it. He didn't want to. He had long ago made his peace with the life he had.

Right. Even with Stavros gone and him stepping up at Theakis Shipping, he still felt like an outsider. Like the spare heir that he'd always been to his father.

He rubbed the back of his neck, feeling the expectations of everyone weighing on him.

"I've got a bottle of pinot grigio that might be a little old, or soda, or light beer."

He shook his head. "Beer. Thank you."

She got him a drink and then sat down next to him with a can of diet soda in front of her. "We have a lot of details to iron out. I'll let them know at work that I'm leaving. I really don't think they'll be able to find a replacement by next week. Could you delay your departure until the following week?"

He could, but he didn't want to. He needed to get out of this place and back to his world. Back to the place where he was in control. But Ava had asked him for little else and he'd seen tonight how necessary she was to integrating Theo into his life. "Yes, I can do that. Tomorrow we'll make arrangements for you and Theo to move into my house."

"Can't we stay here?"

"I think Theo will be more comfortable with you, but if you decide to stay here that's fine."

She stood up and paced around the kitchen. "You can't be a dictator about this. Theo and I can move into your place over the weekend. The school week is just too hard."

He pushed to his feet, coming over to cage her body between his and the counter. "I'm not a dictator, Ava."

"You act like one. I'm not ready to sign over all decision-making rights to you."

"I'm not asking that."

She smelled so damned good, he thought. He couldn't resist lowering his head and inhaling. Wrapping himself in the sweet scent that was Ava.

She shook her head. "You are too used to getting your way."

"Not true," he said. He did like to get his way, but his life had changed and now he was living up to others' expectations. It was true that with Ava he liked to feel in control. It made the entire situation more palatable.

"Liar."

"That's not very nice, Ava."

"You don't think I'm nice," she said softly.

He wasn't getting into that. "You feel nice, *moro mou*."

He lowered his head and pressed his mouth against

hers. Her lips parted and he tasted the saccharine sweetness of the cola she'd drunk. He brushed his tongue over the seam between her lips, keeping the contact light to prove to himself that he was still in control. But he wasn't.

In his mind, he lifted her up on the countertop and pushed her legs apart so he could stand between them. In his mind, he slipped his hand under her sweater and palmed the soft weight of her breasts. In his mind, he was a man who didn't care about the past and was free to give in to the passion that she called from him as effortlessly as the sirens lured sailors.

Ava wasn't sure this was the best idea, but being in Christos's arms was the one thing she couldn't resist. The last few years had been hard as she'd struggled to find her place in the world with Theo. But she was happy with who she was and didn't know whether taking this leap—going to Greece with the one man who'd broken her heart—was the right thing to do.

His warm breath brushed her cheek, helping her believe this was right. Exactly what she needed. And then his mouth moved over hers and she stopped thinking. His lips parted and his tongue thrust past the barrier of her teeth, tasting her with long languid strokes.

She slid her hands up over his shoulders, clinging to him as his mouth moved over hers. She remembered this of Greece and Christos: the warmth of his skin, the possessiveness of his hands on her body.

His hands swept down her back, clutching at her hips

and lifting her up against him. Off-balance, she clung to him as his mouth moved over hers. He lifted her up onto the countertop and stepped between her legs, spreading them farther apart with his hips.

The movement reminded her of where they were and that she didn't exactly trust Christos. She lifted her head, stared down at him in the revealing illumination of the recessed fluorescent lights.

"I…I'm not ready for this," she said, carefully trying to calm the flush of arousal running through her veins. She couldn't resist running her fingers through his thick silky hair.

"You feel ready," he said. He ran one finger down the line of her jaw to her neck, sweeping slowly down to rest on the pulse beating frantically at the base.

"That's a chemical reaction," she said, gathering her wits a little bit at a time.

"So?"

"Christos—"

He rubbed his other thumb over her lips. "I've missed the sound of my name on your lips."

She shuddered and leaned into him. She rested her head on his shoulder, because she didn't want to see his eyes and maybe glimpse the truth—that this was just a line to get her into his bed, except, when had he ever had to lure her there? She'd wanted him from the first moment she'd stepped off the private plane on Mykonos and seen him.

Even Nikki had noticed and warned her away from

her brother-in-law. Reminded her in that forceful way of hers that Ava's responsibility was to Nikki's children.

She stiffened in Christos's arms and pushed away. "Are you really going to marry me or is that just a ploy to get me to cooperate?" she asked.

Christos kept his hands on her waist holding her steady even though she tried to draw away. "You'll just have to wait and see, won't you?"

"Christos—"

"Don't question me, Ava. You'll have to trust what I've told you. There is nothing you can say that will make me change my mind."

"I *can* make this difficult for you," she said, after a long moment. She hated that this issue of trust was between them. There could never be peace between them until he acknowledged he'd been wrong five years ago.

"You're welcome to try, but I fight hard and always win."

"Funny. I would have said our first match-up ended in a draw. Did pushing me out of your life and accusing me of infidelity feel like a win to you?"

He cursed. Then leaned down so close that their noses touched. "Don't bring up the past or I'll take Theo out of here and never look back."

She felt a frisson of fear and tears stung her eyes. The thought of losing her son was more than she could bear.

Christos cursed again and drew her back into his arms. "Sorry."

"For?"

"Being a bastard. I don't want to talk about the past with you. I can't forgive what you did or how things ended between us."

His arms were gentle around her and she wondered at the contradiction of this man. She was afraid to trust and at the same time afraid not to. Despite the fact that he had that icy control over his emotions, she could feel the fire beneath the surface.

She blinked to try to stop the tears that were burning in her eyes, but they fell anyway, flowing down her cheeks.

"I'm not going to take your son away," he said.

"We could have a DNA test," she said at last. She'd resisted having one originally, because she'd gone to Christos a virgin; he should have understood that she would never give her body so easily to another. And she wanted his trust. What woman in love didn't want her man to trust her?

"That's not necessary. Theo is of Theakis blood, that is enough."

She nodded against his shoulder, suddenly very tired. Christos tipped her head up and thumbed away the tracks of her tears.

Then he brushed his lips over hers. "Let's start anew."

She nodded. Yes, starting anew sounded good to her. Christos left a short while later and she tried to tell herself that they'd resolved the past, but a part of her knew they hadn't. She hoped leaving it be would be enough, but experience had taught her that incidents from the past always came back to haunt her.

Four

The muted sounds coming from the nursery enticed Christos out of his office. The singing was off-key and the words undistinguishable, but the joy…he could hear it all the way downstairs.

He was tempted to leave the work he really didn't want to do and go upstairs and join them—the boy he'd claimed as his heir and the woman…the woman he wanted to claim as his own.

Ten days shouldn't change a man's life, he thought, yet that was exactly what had happened. It was ten days since he'd seen *her* again. Since he'd met Theo for the first time and wished for things he'd never wanted.

His mobile phone rang. The last thing he wanted to

do was talk to anyone. When he glanced at the caller ID screen and saw it was his father, he was tempted to let it go to voice mail, but the old man would simply call Antonio and force Christos to take the call.

"Hello, *patera*."

"Why haven't you called?" Ari Theakis asked. Straight to business. The old man wasn't exactly known for his emotional outbursts. That might be why Christos had given in when his father, lying in a hospital bed, had begged him to take over where Stavros had left off.

"Was I supposed to?"

"Yes. Have you seen my grandson?"

"Yes. He's living with me." Living with Theo and Ava was different than he'd expected it to be. Now that they were here, he'd realized how empty his homes had always been. Unlike the servants and paid staff that usually inhabited his residences, Theo and Ava didn't leave him alone. One or the other was always popping into his office and inviting him to do something—watch TV, read a book, play with Rescue Heroes.

"Good. When will you be bringing him home?"

"Soon," he said. The timetable for their departure had been delayed by Ava's replacement, who needed another week before she could take over the class and Ava had told him she didn't want to make her class go through an adjustment twice, which they would have to do if a substitute was brought in now.

He'd had to respect that request. So they were still

in Florida. "We need a legal heir now. I don't like the thought of the Theakis line ending with you."

"Believe me, *patera*, I'm well aware of that," Christos said. Theo had to be declared Christos's heir before the annual board meeting in the fall. Otherwise another branch of the Theakis extended family could take control of the shipping line if anything happened to Christos, something his father didn't want and even Christos agreed would be a bad thing. His Uncle Tony didn't have the best head for business. But then, he'd been a second son, just like Christos.

"What about the girl?"

"Ava?" The last thing he wanted to do was talk about her with his father.

"Yes."

"What about her?"

"Don't play with me, boy. I'm still the head of this family."

"She'll be coming home with me. She refused to relinquish her rights to the boy." He was glad about that. Reveled in the fact that Ava was a really good mother. He had a hard time reconciling what he knew about her with the person she was today. Maybe she had changed when she became a mother, as she'd said.

"Is that wise? We don't trust her."

"*Patera*, you asked me to take over and to bring home an heir before the board of directors held their emergency meeting. I'm doing it and I'll do it my way. If you don't like it, I'm happy to go back to my other business interests."

Actually, that solution would be for the best. Ava and Theo could go back to their lives, and he could return to the world he knew. No more long hours running a shipping line and feeling his brother's presence each time he entered the office.

There was silence on the line and Christos had no doubt his father was wishing that Stavros hadn't died in that plane crash. Who knew, maybe he was even thinking that a swap would have been better. Christos in Stavros's place. But even Ari didn't have control over life and death and Christos was now the only Theakis brother.

"I have to go. I'll have Antonio send our travel plans once they are in place."

"Are you marrying the girl?"

"Yes, I am."

"Good. The boy will need siblings."

"*Patera…*"

"The wedding should take place here on Mykonos. I'll have Maria see to the arrangements," Ari continued, making plans to rule Christos's life.

"Have her call Ava. I'll give Antonio those numbers."

He hung up. Suddenly the library felt too small. He walked out onto the patio and stood there in the shadows of the early evening. His father always made him feel as if…as if he wasn't good enough. Even now, when he was doing Ari's bidding, there was a part of him that knew he was always second-best. The son least likely to become what his father wanted.

"Christos?"

He glanced over his shoulder. Ava stood in the doorway to the living room. She wore a pair of black leggings that made her legs look a mile long. She had a long-sleeved T-shirt on, and she looked so comfortable and approachable. She was relaxed in his home, and he wasn't.

"Yes?"

"Do you want to join us for story time?"

Story time? This was what his life was becoming. If Gui and Tristan could see him, they'd never let him live it down. But his friends weren't here. Only Ava and Theo and the house staff.

The thing was, he wanted to join them. He wanted to go up those stairs and sit on the pile of pillows that Ava had stacked in the corner and listen to her sweet voice telling tales where parents didn't have expectations that could never be met. And brothers didn't die. And princesses were really pretty and sweet and true.

"You okay?"

"Yes. I have a lot of work to do."

"Oh. Um…okay."

But it didn't seem okay to him.

"What is it?"

"Theo wanted to hear the ending of the tale you were telling him when he fell asleep last night. The one about some sea monster."

Ava'd had an obligation to attend a function at her school and he'd found himself alone with the boy. "Let me tie up a few details down here and then I'll be up."

She nodded and turned away, but then came back. "Thanks for all you're doing with Theo."

He smiled. He liked the boy. As much as Theo looked like a Theakis, it was obvious to Christos that he had Ava's personality. He was very curious about everything, but cautious at the same time. Christos rubbed his hand over his eyes and looked up at the sky, seeking the familiar pattern of the stars. But it didn't sooth him.

He wanted Ava. That was the cause of the restlessness in him. Not the long hours spent working at Theakis Shipping or the fact that he had a new heir he was getting to know.

There was a restless yearning in him for her, and having her in his home but not in his bed was winding him too tight.

Ava tried to relax into the cushions but this close to Christos, she couldn't. Theo was tucked up between the two of them with Christos's arm draped over them both. His earthy cologne filled each breath she took.

His profile was sculptured and classical. One look at him and there was no doubt that he was Greek. His thick ebony hair and dark olive skin...

"Ava?"

"Hmm?"

"You're staring at me," he said.

She flushed. "Just thinking how much you look like Theo."

He arched one eyebrow at her, clearly letting her know that he wasn't buying her somewhat flimsy excuse. She shrugged.

He continued the story he was telling. She loved the deep cadence of his voice. She leaned back against the pillows, closing her eyes for just a minute, and drifted to sleep without realizing it, waking only when she heard the soft sounds of Theo's whisper.

"She can sleep with me, *Baba*."

"Should I carry her to your bed?"

Ava forced her eyes open. "Did I miss the end of the story?"

"Yes," Theo said. "I've already brushed my teeth."

Ava glanced up at Christos, who shrugged his shoulders. "We didn't want to wake you."

"Thanks for helping him with his nighttime routine."

"No problem," he said, rubbing his hand over Theo's head. "Let's get you tucked in."

Ava braced one hand on the floor to get up. Christos offered his hand and tugged her to her feet. The strength behind his tug knocked her off balance, and she fell against his hard chest. He wrapped an arm around her waist for a second before letting her go.

God, she wanted this man. She wished that life were simpler. That she was more sure of herself and the decision she'd made to go to Greece. Then she'd be unafraid of taking a chance on acting on the passion between them.

"Come on, Mama. Prayer time."

They tucked Theo in and she and Christos left the room together. The moment was surreal in that she'd spent so many years imagining what it would be like to have Christos in their lives, and here he was. But she knew they were both just playacting for the sake of their son.

She closed the door leading to the hallway, leaving it open a crack the way she always did. It was early, and too soon to retreat to her suite of rooms just yet. Now that she'd had her little power nap, she needed…wanted to get to know Christos.

Their summer affair had been full of hidden rendez-vous and secret embraces. As nanny to Stavros and Nikki's daughters, she'd been part of the staff, and Christos…well he'd been busy away from Mykonos during the week, flying in on the weekends and sweeping her off to his yacht the minute her shift with the girls ended. Feeding her exotic foods, telling her tales of the sea and making love to her.

She followed him down the stairs into the formal living room. He went to the wet bar and poured two fingers of Scotch into a glass.

"We need to talk," Christos said.

"About?"

"Theo's religion. We're all Greek Orthodox. I'd like you both to convert."

"Ah… I'll think about it," she said, religion having not

been on her mind. "I was hoping we could spend some time together tonight and get to know each other better."

"Doing what?"

She wasn't sure. She'd been sneaking around to see Christos during their torrid affair and she had no idea what he usually did with his free time. On Mykonos he'd talked of little besides the passion that flowed so powerfully between them.

"I don't know. Watch a game, or talk, or whatever it is that you like to do."

"Come over here, Ava," he said.

She took a few steps into the room and then realized that she wasn't being herself. She was still stuck in the past when it came to Christos. She wasn't as shy as he always made her feel. Pushing aside the doubts that had been brought on by the way things had ended between them, she sank down onto the white leather couch. "You come here."

He arched one eyebrow at her in that totally arrogant way of his.

He poured himself another drink and came over to her side. Sprawling out on the couch, stretching his free arm along the back, he took a sip of his drink and just watched her.

"Now what?"

She thought about it. Somehow she had the idea that telling him to take off his shirt wasn't going to really help her quest to know more about the man he'd become. But it would satisfy her curiosity.

"Ava, you're staring again."

"I can't help it. There's a part of me that can't believe you're really here."

She realized she'd surprised him when he stiffened on the couch.

"Staring at me helps?"

"No. I stare at you because…" She took a deep breath. "Because you're incredibly attractive and I've always liked looking at you."

He leaned forward, putting his glass on the coffee table. "That's good."

"Is it?"

"We're going to be married," he said.

"Is this going to be a real marriage?" she asked.

He pushed to his feet. "I'm not interested in being married to an unfaithful woman."

"I'm not interested in any man but you, Christos. I never have been."

He looked at her. "If you even look at another man…"

The jealousy she remembered. And she had no way to combat it. He had to trust her. And she had to show him that he could. "I'm only looking at you."

"Prove it."

"How?"

"Come to me," he said, holding his hand out to her.

Ava was the only woman in the world who evoked such deep feelings in him. Feelings that made him volatile. And he hated that.

"I don't see what that will prove," she said, nervously tucking a strand of hair behind her ear.

He just kept his hand extended toward her and waited. It was time to set the boundaries of the relationship and to let her know in no uncertain terms exactly who was in charge.

Finally she pushed to her feet and took a few steps toward him. He loved the way she moved. There was something distinctly feminine in the way her hips swayed with each step she took.

"I'm here, now what?"

He shook his head and waited for her to close the gap between them. She placed her hand in his and he drew her closer until their chests brushed.

"Now tip your head back," he said.

He wished he could say that he was in complete control but he wasn't. He wanted this woman with the kind of passion that shouldn't have been possible because he didn't trust her. Yet a part of him did. He trusted this reaction from her.

Her head fell back and their eyes met. He forgot about games and proving anything when he saw that look in her eyes. He lowered his head to hers, intending to stake a claim with his kiss, but when her lips parted under his, he forgot about plans and games.

"Excuse me, sir."

Christos didn't take his eyes off Ava. "Not now, Antonio."

"Mr. Sabina is on the phone and he said it was urgent."

Damn. He dropped his arms and stepped away from Ava. "I'll take the call in my study."

Antonio nodded and left the room. Ava had one arm wrapped around her waist. The fingers of her other hand moved slowly over her lips. "May I come with you?"

He started to say no but then just shrugged. "It's business so it might be boring."

"That's okay. I want to know what you do, try to understand it."

He couldn't imagine why that would be something she'd be interested in. He was very aware of her presence behind him as they walked down the hall to his study. She sat in one of the large brown leather guest chairs as he went behind the desk. He picked up the phone.

"What's up, Tristan?"

"Vincent Perez has been embezzling. I realize that it's late at night where you are, but we're going to need to deal with this in the morning."

"Do you need me back in London?" he asked. The corporate offices for Seconds nightclubs were located there. And maybe some distance and time away from Ava would help him get his head back in the game and away from how tempting she was.

"No. Gui is taking care of pressing charges. He was the closest. But we're going to have to look at the rest of the finance staff and find a suitable replacement for Vincent. Are you available at nine your time tomorrow?"

Christos palmed his BlackBerry from his pocket and checked his calendar. "Yes."

"How are things going with the woman?" Tristan asked.

"Good."

"Good?"

"We're almost ready to return to Greece, and then I think all the details will straighten out."

"Ah, is she there with you?"

"Yes."

"Did I interrupt anything?"

"*Au revoir,* Tris."

"I did," Tristan said, still laughing as Christos disconnected the call.

Ava watched him with those wide blue eyes of hers. "What's in London?"

He didn't want to talk business with her, but maybe it was better than the alternative—lifting her out of that chair and into his arms.

"A business venture I have with a couple of friends." When they'd started Seconds, they'd been twenty and defiant, each refusing to follow in the predestined path his family had outlined for him. Tristan's family was in publishing on a big scale. And Guillermo—well, Gui's family were royal and they didn't approve of owning something so base as a chain of provocative nightclubs.

"I don't know any of your friends," she said, quietly.

"Why would you?"

"We were intimate with each other, Christos, shouldn't we know at least a few of the people who are important in each other's life?"

He rubbed the back of his neck, wondering if that was why she'd turned to Stavros. Was it because he'd insulated her from everyone else? He didn't want to dwell on the need he'd had to make her completely his, to become her entire world.

"We were lovers, Ava, little more."

"Now we are parents and you want us to marry."

"I believe you want that, too," he said, unsure where she was going with this. He tried not to think about what she'd said about Theo. He let the boy call him *Baba*, because to tell him not to would have been awkward, but he didn't believe he was the boy's father.

"I can't be married to a stranger. Not even for Theo's sake."

"What do you want from me?"

She pursed her lips as she thought. Always so cautious, this one was. "I want a chance to become friends with you. I don't know a lot of happily married couples, but the ones I do know…well, they are friends with each other. I think Theo deserves that from us."

He nodded. It was one of the reasons he'd offered to marry her instead of just taking Theo back to Greece. "That's amicable to me."

"You have to stop trying to make everything between us sound like business."

"Why do I have to do that?"

"Because it makes me want to slap you when you do it."

"I didn't realize you have violent tendencies."

"Only with you, Christos," she said.

He walked around his desk and leaned against it so that only a few feet of space separated them. "Business is the only way I know how to manage this."

"Manage what?"

The way he felt about her, but he couldn't say that. "Marriage."

"This is a marriage of convenience?"

"It is convenient for both of us," he said.

She rolled her eyes. "I think we should try to be friends."

"How do you propose we do this?"

"Have dinner with some of my friends tomorrow night," she said.

He glanced at his calendar. "I can do an earlier dinner. Perhaps around seven?"

"That's fine."

"Who will we be dining with?" he asked, wanting to run a background check on them to ensure they were the right type of people for Ava to be associating with.

"Laurette Jones and her fiancé, Paul Briscoe." She stared up at him.

"You're staring again."

She flushed. "Will we be lovers?"

"We will be married."

"I can't be intimate with someone who doesn't trust me."

"You were before."

"I'm different now."

Yes, she was. There was an inner strength and core to her that the girl she'd been hadn't had. Before, she'd been a kitten who'd come when called. Now she was a tigress who might come when he called or might turn on him with her claws bared.

And he'd had no idea that the differences in her would make him want her more than ever.

Five

Mykonos was exactly as she'd remembered it. Bright, whitewashed buildings seemed to sparkle from the hills over the deep blue Aegean Sea. Theo's little hand in hers gave her the strength to step off the plane when she saw Ari Theakis waiting for them. Christos's father had never liked her and the situation with Stavros and Christos hadn't exactly helped.

To be honest, she'd been intimidated by the man from the first moment she'd met him. He carried himself with the kind of arrogance that could only be honed in confidence and self-security. Even confined to a wheel-chair, now, he still exuded that arrogance and power.

That utter self-confidence was something she wanted

for Theo, and even if she wasn't still attracted to Christos she would have accepted his offer of marriage in the hopes that living in his presence and the presence of Ari would somehow rub off on Theo and give him that.

"Come on, Mama."

"Be careful going down the stairs," she said.

"I'm not a baby," he reminded her, bounding down the stairs and stopping in front of Ari.

"What are you waiting for?" Christos asked from behind her.

"Your father doesn't like me."

"He doesn't like many people, it's not personal."

"You know what I mean," she said.

Christos put his hand on her shoulder. "You can't change his mind about the past, but you can influence how he sees you in the future."

"You think so?"

"Yes. And he will be grateful to you for giving him a grandson."

She glanced back at Ari in his wheelchair, an attendant close behind him. Theo was standing in front of him, shuffling his feet around and looking a little nervous.

Ava hurried down the stairs to her son's side but before she reached him, Ari reached out to Theo and pulled him into his arms.

She stopped for a moment, seeing what Christos had meant just moments ago—the intense love this man had for her son. He hugged Theo tightly to him and buried his face in Theo's thick black hair.

Ava was touched and turned away to give Ari the privacy he needed to deal with his feelings. Christos slipped his arm around her shoulders. "You okay?"

"Yeah. I forgot Ari was human."

"What did you think he was?"

"Some kind of demigod," she said, only half in jest.

"He just thinks he is."

"It's about time you got here." The husky voice had them turning back toward Ari and Theo.

"*Patera*, it's good to see you, too," Christos said, dropping his arm and walking over to his father. Theo stepped back from Ari and came to her side. She glanced at the three males, unable to miss the striking resemblance between them.

"Mr. Theakis, it's good to see you again."

"Ms. Monroe, I see you are back."

She tried to smile, but that wasn't exactly a *Welcome to Mykonos*. "Yes I am. Theo and I are very excited to be here."

"It is good that you brought the boy. He needs to learn to be a proper Theakis."

He turned his wheelchair around before she could respond and headed toward the limo, attendant hurrying in his wake. Clearly he wasn't interested in developing any kind of friendship with her. In the past he'd treated her as a servant...which, as the nanny for Althea and Venni, she had been. But she'd hoped...ah, who cared what a cantankerous old man thought.

"Mama, Grandfather said he's prepared a special room just for me to play in."

"That will be nice, won't it?" Ava asked her son, wondering if she was going to find herself, like Nikki Theakis, relegated to the status of an observer in her own child's life. She shook her head, vowing not to let that happen.

"Yes." Theo curled his hand around hers, holding it tightly in his grip.

As Christos and his father talked next to the waiting limo, she stooped so she was on Theo's level. "What's up?"

"He held me really tight, Mama."

"He's just happy to see you."

"That's what he said. I'm glad he likes me."

"Of course he likes you. Everyone likes you."

"Is everything okay?" Christos asked, striding back from Ari.

"Yes," she said, standing up.

"Please, come. I have a meeting at the office in a little over an hour. You can ride back to the house with my father."

"You're not coming with us?"

"Not right now. I'll see you both later."

Ava tried not to feel that she was being abandoned, which was a silly feeling anyway. But she didn't really know Ari and he didn't seem to be looking forward to getting to know her better.

Christos lifted Theo in his arms, said something that only the two of them could hear and gave him a hug and kiss. When he set Theo on his feet her son ran over to the limo and climbed into the long black car.

"I'll see you at dinner."

She nodded.

He turned to walk away then paused. "Are you sure you're okay?"

"I will be. It's just…"

"What?"

"I don't have many fond memories of my last glimpse of this airport. It's like…" She shook her head. She wasn't going to tell him that everything was coming back to her. The overwhelming anger and fear. She had been so afraid when she'd realized she was pregnant and on her own.

"Everything's different this time," Christos said.

"You're right. I'm being silly. I think I'm tired from all the traveling."

"I expect you are," Christos said. "You have my mobile number?"

"Yes."

"Call me if you need anything," he said.

"But your meeting…" she said.

"Today I can make time for you. If I'd planned our arrival better I would have saved the day for you and Theo."

The chaotic feelings from the past started to melt away as she realized that things really were different this time and Christos was going to be by her side. She'd been alone for so long; it was hard to accept that she wasn't anymore, especially when what she usually saw of Christos was his back as he walked away.

The room that Ari had prepared for Theo was every child's dream. It was actually a suite of three rooms, the sleeping quarters sumptuously painted so that it seemed you were in the middle of the Aegean Sea with the bed a big sailboat in the middle. The mural on the wall started with the sunrise, continued around the room to the big bay windows that overlooked the lushly land-scaped back garden and then, on the other side of the window, night fell and stars filled the sky.

"This room is…"

"Fitting for the Theakis heir," Ari said from the doorway.

"Yes it is. Thank you for doing so much for my son."

"I didn't do it for *your* son, Ms. Monroe, I did it for my heir."

"Mr. Theakis…"

He went to the adjacent room before she could say anything else. Damn. She hated the way he kept dis-missing her.

She followed him into the playroom, which was almost bigger than her entire little house in Florida. Theo stood in the middle of the room just staring at everything. He couldn't tell where to start first in his play. Finally he just sat down in the middle of the room and looked up at her.

"Mama? Where's my Rescue Heroes?"

"I'll get them."

"While your mother goes to get those things, let me show you this area, Theo. I had a state-of-the-art plasma-screen TV installed for you. Each morning you will watch your lessons in Greek history and the history of the Theakis family."

Ava paused in the doorway. "Mr. Theakis, we need to talk before you plan out Theo's days."

"I'm not planning his days, Ms. Monroe, I'm teaching him to be a proper Theakis. Unfortunately those lessons are ones he's been lacking."

Ava glared at the older man. She wanted to say, *Whose fault is that*, but couldn't, not in front of Theo.

"We can discuss this later."

"Check with my secretary and have him put you on my schedule," Ari said and left the room.

Ava grabbed a pillow off the couch in front of the TV and threw it against the wall. Theo grabbed one and did the same, laughing. She started laughing with her son, feeling some of the tension ease out of her.

"Do you want to watch Greek lessons?"

He shrugged. "I do want to be a good Theakis."

"You can't be anything else. You *are* a Theakis."

Theo nodded.

But as the afternoon wore on, she noticed that her son's playing was different. Each time he did anything, he'd stop and ask her if it was proper Theakis behavior, which made her crazy. She left him playing to try to find Ari, but the older man's secretary told her that Ari was unavailable…for the next few weeks.

She'd vowed to fight Ari, to ensure that she was in charge of Theo's upbringing, but how could she when he wouldn't talk to her? She was stymied, unsure how to deal with Christos's father.

She didn't have to, she thought. She and Christos shared responsibility for Theo. She'd give it a few days and if Ari didn't come around, she go to Christos with her concerns.

Christos rubbed the back of his neck and glanced at the clock. Damn, nine o'clock. Time had slipped away from him as he'd been in meeting after meeting. The last week had been completely crazy with meetings and catching up. Theakis Shipping wasn't an easy conglomerate to run and Christos's time was at a premium. He'd called Theo to talk to him before he went to bed but had been unable to get back to the house for dinner.

Theakis Shipping was suffering, thanks to his ignoring it for as long as he had. Everyone seemed to have stopped making decisions when Stavros had died and had been waiting for him to step in. Christos was willing to do just that, but not all in one week.

"We'll finish this in the morning," he declared, and the staff nodded and left the conference room. He left the office without glancing back, fighting the urge to get in his Ferrari and drive to the dock where he kept his yacht and then leave Mykonos and Theakis Shipping far behind.

The house was quiet when he entered it. He paused at the landing on the second floor, glancing to the wing on the left where he knew his father had assigned rooms to Theo and Ava. He needed to turn right and go to his quarters.

He scrubbed his hand over his face and forced himself to his rooms. The door leading to his balcony was open and a cool breeze flowed in. He dropped his briefcase on one of the chairs in the sitting area.

As soon as he stepped out onto the balcony he knew that he wasn't alone.

"Good evening, Ava."

She turned from the railing. She wore a long, flowing skirt that shifted around her legs with the breeze and a thin summer sweater that hugged the curves of her breasts. "I've been waiting for you."

"Why?" he asked, trying to fight the urge to scoop her up in his arms and carry her into his bedroom.

"I wanted to talk to you."

"Can it wait until morning?" he asked.

"It could if I thought I'd see you at breakfast."

He'd been out of the house before dawn every morning since they'd arrived on Mykonos. "My schedule is demanding."

"I know," she said. "That's why I'm here."

"What's up?"

"It's about Theo and your father."

"Is he too sharp with Theo?"

"No, nothing like that."

"Then what?"

"He's just so Greek. He's trying to make Theo into a miniature version of him. I don't like it, but he won't listen to me."

Christos could well imagine what Ari was teaching his grandson. "Being a Theakis is an important part of Theo's upbringing. *Patera* is probably just trying to catch him up on everything he's missed in the last few years."

She shook her head. "It's more than that. Every time Theo does something now, he asks me if he's living up to the Theakis name. He's four, Christos. He should be playing, having fun and enjoying life, not worrying about keeping up your family image."

"It will be your family, too, in a few weeks."

"I can understand that, but he's still just a little boy."

"I'll talk to my father and tell him to back off."

"No. I don't want you to do that."

"What do you want then?" he asked.

"Some advice on how I can deal with your father. He keeps telling me that I'm not Greek so I can't understand, and his secretary won't give me any time on his calendar."

She sounded so upset and so earnest that he wanted to fix this for her. But he knew the old man wasn't going to soften in his attitude toward Ava. Even if she'd been a Greek woman, he'd treat her the same way.

"It's just his way. Don't let it bother you."

"I can't help it. All day long he watches me and

everything I do. Then when Theo's out of the room he tells me all the things I'm doing wrong."

Christos walked over to her and pulled her into his arms. She nestled against him as though she belonged there. And for the first time that day, he felt a measure of peace. This was what he'd been missing during the long hours at the Theakis Shipping office. And he knew this was a false promise. Ava wasn't waiting here for him. She'd been waiting for advice. He should drop his arms and move away…except he was wound so tight from wanting her that he'd take whatever he could get.

"That's his way. Just tell him to mind his own business."

She pulled back and glanced up at him. "That might work for you. You get to leave this house."

"Is that what this is all about?"

She shrugged and drew back. "I'm not sure what my life is going to be like as your wife."

"Taking care of Theo and socializing with me in the evenings."

"Oh. I'm just…"

"What, Ava?"

"I don't know. I feel so isolated from everything. I don't want to crowd Theo, but there's no one else here who likes me."

"I like you," he said.

"Really?" she asked.

"Yes, really."

He had the feeling he was getting closer to whatever

was upsetting her. "I…I don't have anyone I can ask to be my attendants in the wedding. I'd like to invite Laurette to be my maid of honor, but she can't afford to fly from Florida. And that still leaves three openings…I know you have three groomsmen, right? Antonio, and then Tristan and Guillermo?"

"I'll arrange it all. I like Laurette and you should have your friends with you. Is there anyone else we should bring over from the States?"

She shook her head.

"Don't worry. I'll have Guillermo and Tristan each draft a woman to bring down the aisle."

"That's not the point," she said.

"What is the point?"

"I'm…not sure I can live here."

He rubbed the back of his neck. "We're to be married in less than two weeks."

"I know. That's why I'm bringing this up now. This last week has given me a glimpse of what my life will be. I need something more to do."

He understood what she meant; even he didn't really like living in the Theakis compound, but certain concessions had to be made. He ran through the job openings they had at Theakis and couldn't think of one thing that was suitable for the mother of the Theakis heir to fill. But then he remembered that Nikki had served on their family's foundation board.

"I've got a few ideas that I'll investigate tomorrow."

"Do you have time for that?"

"No, but I'll make time for you. I want you to be happy here."

Ava knew she needed to leave Christos alone to let him have some rest. He was working very hard; she saw the signs of stress in his eyes and in the way he carried himself. "This probably isn't the best time for you to marry me."

"Is that what this is all about, Ava? You want to back out of the wedding?"

"No," she said. "I definitely don't want that. I just don't like seeing you so tense all the time."

He quirked one eyebrow at her. "Why don't we go back into my bedroom and you can help me relax?"

"Sex with you was never relaxing," she said, trying to play off the desire she had to do just that.

"Was it relaxing with my brother?" he asked, with a bit of bite to his words.

She blanched. She'd forgotten he still believed she'd slept with his brother. Stavros had promised her he'd make everything right when she'd signed that agreement years ago, but he never had.

"I told you I never slept with Stavros," she said.

"So you said." He was so Greek at the moment. The fire and passion in him burned beneath that arrogance.

"Christos, you still don't believe me?" She should let this go, but he'd asked her to marry him. How were they going to have a life together if he didn't trust her?

"I don't want to talk about it. I'm not interested in the other lovers you've had."

"There haven't *been* any other lovers," she said. *Only you.* There'd only ever been Christos for her.

She walked over to him and stopped when barely an inch of space separated them. She put her hands on his shoulders and went up on her tiptoes so that she could stare into his obsidian eyes.

"I'm not going to marry you until we resolve this issue."

He shook his head. "Then you may return to the States."

"Christos, stop being impossible. How can I prove to you that Stavros and I were never intimate?"

"You can't," he said.

She turned away so he wouldn't see the tears burning in her eyes. "We have to have trust between us. If we had the DNA test done on Theo…would that convince you that I'm not lying?"

"Ava…you would do that? I thought you wanted me to trust your word on Theo."

"I do. But I can't see how we're ever going to live together as man and wife if I don't prove myself to you."

"You don't have to prove yourself. I'm a jealous man, you know that, right?"

"Yes. But I've never done anything to make you jealous," she said.

"Just seeing you walk into a room and be noticed by another man makes me jealous," he said, putting his hands on her shoulders.

"I only see you," she admitted, tipping her head back on his shoulder.

"*Moro mou*," he said drawing her back into his arms.

Ava stopped thinking the minute her lips touched Christos's. The cool breeze stirred her hair and she burrowed closer to his warmth.

She'd told herself she was here only because of her contentious relationship with his father, no other reason. But as his lips moved over hers, she knew she was a liar.

She was here with Christos because she wanted the man and he'd…he'd been gone too often since they'd arrived in Mykonos. And she'd had second thoughts. Fears that their life together would be like this, this distance always between them. But here was the fire she remembered.

It was hard not to fall for Christos.

He took a halfstep back from her and watched her through half-lidded eyes. He held her wrists loosely in his hands, his gaze moving over her, making her hyper-aware of him and at the same time of her body.

She didn't need to protect herself from the past tonight. She was here with Christos. The man she'd been thinking about too much of the time lately. And damned if she wasn't going to enjoy him.

"Come," he said, drawing her toward the shadowed bedroom.

He was confident, sure of himself, and with plenty of cause. He lowered his head and she held her breath. Brushing his lips over her cheek, he held her close but with that tenderness no one had shown toward her before him.

His long fingers caressed her neck, slow sweeps up and down, until she shivered in his arms. She needed more from him. She grabbed his shoulders and brought her mouth to his.

He sighed her name and took over the kiss. Sliding his arms down her back, he edged her toward the bed. It hit the back of her legs and she sat down. He followed her, never breaking their kiss.

His tongue moved easily with hers, tempting her further, tasting her deeper and making her long for him. Her skin felt too tight. Her breasts were heavy, craving his touch. Between her legs she was moistening for him, ready for him.

Squirming, she shifted around until she was on his lap, her legs straddling him. She lifted her head to look down at him. His skin was flushed, his lips wet from their kisses. She flexed her fingers against his shoulders. He really was solid muscle.

"Do you remember what we used to do?" he asked.

She wanted to laugh at his playfulness. She'd never forgotten the wicked, sexy games they'd often played together. "Mmm, I'm not sure, it's still a little foggy."

"What can I do to remind you?"

She reached for the bedside table and turned on the lamp. In the soft glow of the light she saw that Christos was turned on.

"Could you...take your shirt off?" she said. She'd

been longing to touch his chest since the night he'd lifted her onto her kitchen counter and stepped between her legs.

"Do you think it will help?" he asked, pulling off his tie and tossing it on the comforter of his king-sized bed.

"Definitely," she said.

He reached between them, the backs of his fingers brushing her breasts as he unbuttoned his shirt. She shook from the brief contact and bit her lip to keep from asking for more.

The fabric parted to reveal the tanned skin below. That small gold medallion still hung around his neck. She touched the gold charm. "This I remember."

"Good, I'm glad to know it's coming back to you."

She leaned down and pressed her lips to his chest. He tasted of some male essence that was uniquely Christos. And she hadn't realized how hungry she'd been for him until this moment. She'd been ignoring the fact that she was still a woman and not just Theo's mother for too long.

With Christos, she wanted to revel in her femininity again. She slid her lips over his warm skin. He tunneled his fingers into her hair, directing her head toward his nipple. She knew that he liked to feel the edge of her teeth against that sensitive skin.

To tease them both she let him only have the soft brush of her tongue. "Is this what you want?"

"Ava…"

She made a wondering sound against him, drawing his hard nipple into her mouth. She held him between her teeth and sucked on him. He groaned her name, his hips surging up between her legs.

He was hot and hard and she was ready for him. Maybe because it had been a long time since she'd made love…and of course, her last time had been with him.

Gently, he pulled her head away from his body and lifted her over him. He pushed the sweater she wore out of his way. She had no bra on and the air in the room combined with the heat of his gaze made her nipples bead.

He ran his finger down the center of her body, over her sternum and between her ribs, lingering on her belly button and then stopping at the waistband of her skirt.

He slowly traced the same path upward again. This time his fingers feathered under the full globes of her breasts, coming very close to touching her nipples. A shaft of desire pierced Ava, shaking her.

She needed more. She wanted more. Her heart beat so swiftly and loudly she was sure he could hear it. She scraped her fingernails lightly down his chest. He groaned, the sound rumbling from his chest. He leaned back and braced himself on his elbows.

His muscles jumped under her touch. She circled his nipple then scraped her nail down the center line of his body, following the fine dusting of hair that narrowed and disappeared into the waistband of his pants.

His stomach was rock-hard and rippled when he sat up. He pulled her closer, until the tips of her breasts brushed his chest.

"Ava." He said her name like a prayer, holding her against him.

His hard sex nudged her center and she shifted on him, trying to find a better contact. It was impossible with the layers of cloth between them.

He kissed his way down her neck and bit lightly at the base. She shuddered, clutching at his shoulders, grinding her body harder against him.

His big hands cupped her buttocks and urged her to ride him faster. Guiding her motions against him, he bent his head and his tongue stroked her nipple. Then he suckled her.

Everything in her body clenched. She clutched at Christos's shoulders, rubbing harder and faster against his erection as her climax washed over her. She collapsed against his chest. He held her close.

Ava hugged him to her and closed her eyes, reminding herself that this was just sex. He'd walked away from this once before, leaving her shattered and broken. But, right now, with his strong arms around her, it felt as though she'd found her home.

Six

Ava reached down, stroking Christos through his pants. He was so hard he could feel his pulse between his legs. He was close to losing it all. Not exactly the suave playboy image he liked to maintain, but with Ava all bets were off. They always had been. She was a fire that he'd never been able to control.

He lifted her chin and captured her lips with his. She sighed and wrapped her arms around him. When he looked down at her, tears were visible in her pretty blue eyes.

"What's the matter?"

She shook her head. "Nothing. It's just…I've dreamed of this for so long."

"Making love with me?" he asked. "*Moro mou*, you are easy to please."

"I guess I am," she said. "When it comes to you and Theo, I think I have everything a woman could want."

He felt a twinge of something close to anger at her mention of Theo. Not directed at the boy, but directed at Ava, because he still couldn't accept her insistence that he was the boy's father. And at his brother, because Stavros had known how much Christos was into Ava that summer, and he should have stayed away from her.

"What is it? Why does your face get all tight when I mention Theo?"

"I hate the fact that…"

"That you don't believe that you're his father?"

He lifted her off his body and set her on the bed, no longer in the mood to linger there with her. He reached for his shirt and drew it on as he paced across the room to the wet bar.

"Christos."

"Yes?"

"You must be coming to believe me, right? Why else would you marry me?"

He shook his head. Even he knew better than to tell her that he was marrying her for the Theakis heir and, well, hell, for the sex that had always been incredible between them.

"What will it take to convince you?" she asked at last.

He glanced over his shoulder, noting that she'd drawn her sweater back on. She had her hands on her hips and he knew she was angry with him.

Too damn bad.

He was angry, too. Things had been going well between them. "What the hell difference does it make? Theo is here, I've claimed him and you and I are to be married."

"It makes all the difference in the world. Even *you* must be able to see that. Do you really want to marry a woman who you think is capable of sleeping with you and another man? Your own *brother*?"

"Hell, no. Our prenuptial agreement is specific about what will happen if you do that again."

"Again? I never did it before."

"It's past, Ava, let it go."

"How can I, when you won't?"

"I'm not going to argue this with you."

"You can't walk away from this. I'm not going to let you. If you want me to marry you, if you want Theo to stay here on Mykonos, we need to finish this now."

"How?"

"I guess trusting me is out," she said, nibbling on her lower lip in that sexy way she always did.

"You lied to me," he said. She had lied about several things. Things like who her family was and where she'd come from.

"That was different. My family is nothing like yours. I thought you'd prefer a woman who came from a similar background."

He understood that. Would have forgiven her the tales about her family back in the States if she'd come to him and told him the truth. But instead he'd had to find out about it from Nikki. His sister-in-law had been concerned when she'd learned of his and Ava's affair and had revealed Ava's background check to him. Everything in it suggested that Ava was a poor girl hoping to bag a wealthy husband. Her lies had only confirmed that.

"I was young and I told you the truth eventually."

But it had been too late. He could never believe that she hadn't overheard him and Nikki talking that morning on the terrace.

"It's inconsequential."

"It's *not*. That's the reason you believe I'd sleep with Stavros."

He set down his whiskey glass before he threw it across the room. He hated those images in his head. The ones of Ava and his brother that he'd never been able to erase.

"Enough. Leave this room."

"No."

"No?"

"I'm sure that's a word you don't hear very often but I think you know what it means."

"Ava—"

"Christos, I'm prepared to be very stubborn about this. I want us to have a real marriage, to have a real family with Theo, and we can't if you don't believe me."

"Fine, we'll have a paternity test."

"Now you'd believe a test over my word?" she asked, there was something broken in her voice and though he wanted to pretend it didn't affect him, it did.

"Ava…"

"Forget it. We're not taking a paternity test. I no

longer want to do that. I'm going to convince you that
you're wrong."

"How will you do that? Stavros is dead. I can never ask
my brother about what happened between the two of you."

"You never talked to him about it?"

"No. And he never denied it when we fought over
you." He'd told Stavros they were dead to each other and
had left Mykonos and Greece, spending the majority of
his time traveling to his various businesses and staying
so busy he never had time to feel the gaping wound that
had been left by that action.

"Oh, Christos."

He hated that she might pity him. "How do you mean
to convince me?"

"By letting you see the woman I am. I could never
betray you and I will stop at nothing to prove that to you."

Ava hadn't realized how much Christos had lost after
she'd returned to America. They'd both had their lives
shattered by the lies that Stavros had told, first to Nikki and
then, when Nikki had gone to Christos, to his own brother.

Christos had seen her alone with Stavros on more
than one occasion. She'd been providing a cover for her
boss and his mistress, another lie that she'd contributed
to that at the time had seemed…well, not exactly
harmless, but necessary.

Convincing Christos to trust her was going to be difficult, she didn't kid herself. Not only because of the
seeds of the past but because she was realizing she still

didn't really like who she was at the most basic level. She'd spent her entire life pretending to be someone she wasn't, pretending that the small, run-down trailer she'd grown up in was a large ranch house, for starters.

She'd lied about so much of where she'd come from that she didn't want to face the truth. But it was past time for that. Theo had never met his maternal grandparents and never would. Her father had kicked her out of the trailer when she'd come home pregnant and jobless.

"I don't like where I came from," she said into the quietness. "And I would never have met you if I hadn't created a different background for myself, so I'm not going to apologize for that. Perhaps it would have been better just to keep silent about my family."

"I wouldn't have judged you by your family. But lying about where you came from…I don't understand that. Hell, half the time I'm hoping no one is judging me by my *patera*. He makes me crazy."

She shook her head, allowing a small smile to touch her lips. "That's because all the Theakis men have to have their own way."

"True. But that's not what you were running from."

"No. I grew up in a run-down trailer that sits in the middle of nowhere. We never had any money."

"Money's not important," he said.

"If you have it. If you don't, it's all anyone ever talks about."

"I don't see what this has to do with my trusting you," he said.

She took a deep breath. Of course he wouldn't. She realized in this moment that she had a choice. She could continue to avoid talking about how she'd grown up and never gain Christos's trust, or she could slowly tear down those barriers.

And was there really a choice? She'd had a glimpse of real happiness in Christos's arms when he'd held her and Theo. Taking a deep breath, she said, "I hate that part of my past. It's the root of every lie I ever told, not just to you, but also to myself."

He reached for the whiskey glass on the wet bar countertop and poured himself another drink. He picked it up and swallowed it quickly. "You lie to yourself?"

"Don't you?"

He shook his head. "No. I face all my failings constantly. They are at times a running litany in my mind."

"What failings?"

He shrugged. "Let's keep this about you."

"We can't have a relationship if I'm the only one who talks."

"We can start with you. Once you've…how did you put it? Ah, yes, once you've let me see the woman you are, then we can delve into my psyche."

"You can be an arrogant jerk," she said.

"So I've been told."

"I don't have many things that mean much to me," she said. "Only my son and then this glimpse of a real relationship with you…"

She had no idea what else to say. She wanted to be

witty and funny and charm him out of his arrogance but she suspected she'd never be able to do that.

She heard him set down his glass, then his footsteps echoed on the tiled floor as he walked toward her. She couldn't believe they'd just shared an explosive sexual encounter on the bed and now they were immersed in this conversation, embroiled in a past that, no matter how fast she ran or how many twists and turns she forced her life to take, still held her trapped.

He stopped in front of her, and she had a glimpse of his bare chest under the shirt that he'd not rebuttoned. She wished she'd just stayed there in his arms.

"Look at me," he said.

She glanced up, surprised to see a very serious look in his eyes. "What?"

"I'm only arrogant when someone really strikes a chord deep inside me. I don't know how to deal with genuine emotion, and you have always made me feel more than I'm comfortable with."

She had no response to that.

He cupped her cheek and she stood very still, afraid she was going to say something that would drive him back across the room.

"I think the reason I felt so betrayed by you is enmeshed in that. If it had been any other woman, I would have just moved on, but you…you have always made me feel like I'm really alive."

Tears burned her eyes and she knew she was right to push for this trust between them. "Me, too."

He dropped his hand and stepped back. "So how do you see this working?"

She blinked her eyes to clear the tears away. "We should spend time together, and not just to talk about the past. Get to know each other again."

"I think we made a start tonight," he said, nodding to the bed behind her.

She nibbled on her lower lip. "Uh, I think we should stay out of bed until we're married. We know we're sexually compatible and I think that just complicates things."

"Sex never complicates things."

"For you, maybe. For me, it makes me want to just curl up in your arms and say to hell with the rest of the world, and that's not any way to solve problems."

Christos poured himself another drink. "Fine. No sex until we're married."

"Do you think you'll trust me by then?"

"I have no idea, but being married does grant me the privilege of your bed and I don't intend to deny myself."

Two weeks, she thought. Could she change his mind in that time?

Theo woke Ava by running into her bedroom and jumping on the bed. His little voice was loud and filled with joy. She'd never really been a cheerful morning-person, but when faced with Theo's grin she couldn't help but smile back at him.

"What are you so excited about?" she asked him. He

was dressed and had on a pair of sandals that Ari had given him when they'd arrived. The shoes were traditional Greek ones that even Ari wore.

"*Baba*. He's going to take us out on his boat today."

"He is?" she asked. She hoped that Christos knew what he was doing. Promising to make time for Theo was one thing; actually promising to take him out on the boat was something else. She didn't want to see Theo disappointed if Christos had to stay late at the office.

"Yes. As soon as you get up. I've been awake for a long time now."

"I'm sorry, sweetheart. Give me a minute to wash my face and I'll be downstairs for my coffee and we can talk about this."

"You don't have to do that. *Baba* is bringing you your coffee."

"He is?" She didn't want to see Christos until she had a chance to comb her hair and brush her teeth. She was about to toss back the covers and make a run for the bathroom.

"I told him…" Theo trailed off. She could guess what her chatty little son had said. Something about Mommy being cranky until she had her first cup of coffee.

She ruffled his hair and drew him close for a hug. "Did you tell him I need coffee first thing?"

Theo nodded against her neck, hugging her back. "Yes, he did."

She glanced up at Christos, who stood in the doorway holding a mug of coffee in each hand. He wore a pair of casual white trousers and a black T-shirt. He looked as if he'd had a good night's sleep, something she envied him.

He came into her room and handed her one of the mugs. She tried to pat down her hair, which was probably flat on one side and sticking straight out on the other. She took a sip of the coffee and tried to play it cool.

"What's this about a boat?"

Christos leaned against the dresser in the corner and sipped his coffee. "After our conversation last night, I decided to take the day off and invite you both to join me on my yacht."

"I thought we were going on a boat," Theo said.

"A yacht is a name for a big boat."

"Oh. How big?"

"Big enough," Christos said. "Would you like to join us, Ava?"

"Yes. I'd like that."

"Good. We'll get out of your hair and wait for you downstairs."

Theo gave her a sloppy kiss and a hug and ran out the door. Christos paused in the doorway.

"Are you sure about this? Taking a day off work?"

"You said something last night that made sense."

"Only one thing?" she asked. Actually she was surprised anything she'd said made sense. She'd been flying blind, driven by emotion, and that never boded well for making sense.

"Well, the not-sleeping-together thing is insane."

She flushed. "Depends on your point of view."

"I'm going to change yours on that topic. But I was referring to when you said that you couldn't build a relationship by yourself."

"I'm glad you were listening," she said.

He put his coffee mug down on the dresser and walked back to the bed. He sat down next to her, his lean hip pressing against her body.

"I always listen," he said.

"I hope so," she said. She'd pinned her hopes for a happy future on the fact that one day he'd really hear her say that she hadn't betrayed him and believe her.

He traced his finger along the line of the sheet where she had it clutched to her chest. "What are you sleeping in?"

She shook her head. "I think we'll leave that to your imagination."

He fingered the cap sleeve of her shirt. "I think we shouldn't. I'm picturing you naked."

"Clearly I'm not."

"Pity."

"Sometimes Theo gets scared at night and sleeps with me."

He ran his finger down the edge of the scoop neck of her pajama top. "What scares him?"

She struggled to keep focused on the conversation and not the feel of his finger moving over her skin. "Different things. He can't always recall."

"Do you always soothe him?"

"Yes. We pray and I sing to him."

"That's one of the things I admire about you," he said.

"What?"

"The way you mother Theo. You're very good with him."

When he'd first been born, she'd been surprised at how much she loved her son. Having him had added a dimension to her life that she'd never realized was missing. He gave her someone to love and on whom to pour all the caring she'd hidden away for years.

"He's easy to love."

"Yes, he is," Christos said. He leaned toward her and she lifted herself up to him. "Are you sure about this no-sex rule?"

She shook her head.

"*Baba*, come on. She'll take all day to get ready if you don't leave her room."

Christos dropped a quick kiss on her lips and stood, picking up his coffee mug on the way out of the room. As the door closed behind the two Theakis males, Ava pulled the covers over her head and tried not to let her heart believe that today was the start of a new life with Christos and Theo.

Seven

Christos eyed his father as the old man maneuvered his wheelchair down the stone ramp leading to the garages. Theo, dancing around him with all that energy, gave Christos something to focus on, but he couldn't turn his mind away from the fact that his father was heading his way. Absently he noted the watergun in Theo's hand.

The conversation last night with Ava still played in his mind. Hell, everything from last night was vivid, especially the way she'd moved against him. The way her soft skin had felt pressed to his.

"Baba?"

"Yes, Theo."

"Is Grandfather coming with us?"

"I didn't invite him," Christos said under his breath, but then his father wasn't really one to wait to be asked. "Why don't you go ask him?" Christos suggested.

Theo ran toward Ari, and Christos went back to packing the things they'd need for a day on the boat. He'd slept little the night before. Once Ava had left his rooms he'd gone to the study and worked all night so that taking the day off wouldn't be a problem.

He didn't exactly hate his new life, but he wasn't sure it was his yet. And Ava's conversation last night had driven home to him the fact that it was past time for him to start figuring out what this new life was going to be.

"You have a call at the main house," Ari said as he came into the garage.

"From whom?"

"Tristan. He said he needed to speak to you this morning. He's on his mobile."

Theo was standing at the back of Ari's wheelchair. He held his water gun in one hand at the ready and scanned the lawn. Christos knew that the boy was pretending to be a bodyguard. He'd played this game with Theo a few days ago.

"Is it safe for you to leave your grandfather and come to the house with me?"

"No, sir. I'd better stay here."

Christos ruffled the boy's hair as he strode past him back toward the main house. Antonio was waiting in the foyer with Christos's BlackBerry.

"Your father insisted on going after you."

"No problem. Did you have a chance to talk to Tristan?"

"No. But he left you a voice mail and a fax is coming through in the study. Do you want me to call Captain Platakis and tell him that you will be delayed?"

"Not yet," Christos said. He didn't want to break his plans with Theo and Ava.

Christos went down the hall into his study and glanced at the fax coming through. More embezzlement business. He dialed Tristan's number.

"Sabina here."

"Tris, it's me."

"Sorry. I'm a bit distracted. We're on a charter flight to Mykonos."

"Why?"

"Need your signature on a few documents."

"The ones that you faxed?"

"Yes. They are the formal charges we're filing against Vincent. I've also sent you the résumés of the three candidates we're considering promoting."

Christos pulled the pages from the machine and started scanning them. "You and Gui make the choice."

"So it's started."

"What?"

"You're not going to be an active partner in Seconds now that you're running the shipping line."

"Don't be ridiculous. I have plans for the day that I can't set aside. If this can wait until evening…"

"What plans?"

"Plans."

"The kind that involve a woman?"

He didn't answer, but that didn't stop Tris.

"From your silence, it sounds serious. Which is why we are coming to you."

"Tristan, I don't interfere in your love life," Christos said.

"I don't have one that lasts more than one night."

"Exactly. Leave me be."

"We just want to meet her. You knew we were coming."

"I'm not going to be on the island today," Christos said.

"We'll find you."

"Somehow I thought you would. I'll leave Antonio at the Theakis compound, he'll prepare your regular quarters."

"Where does Ava stay?"

"In the main house with Theo."

"How is the boy? Is he your son?"

Christos was starting to wonder if Theo was really his son. Christos knew he should just ignore Ava's wishes and have the DNA test conducted, but he wanted…he wanted a chance at something more than the kind of marriage of convenience most of his colleagues had.

Tristan had married for love and against his family's wishes, and for a few brief years had been the happiest man that Christos had ever known. Then his wife had passed away, a victim of cancer.

"What was it like?" he asked.

"What was what like?"

"Being married to Cecile."

Tristan cleared his throat and didn't answer for a moment. "Heaven. Is that what you're searching for?"

"I don't know that I am, but I want a chance at that."

Tristan cleared his throat again. "I hope you find it. With Ava and Theo. You deserve that kind of happiness."

Christos recognized sadness and resignation in Tristan's voice. "You can have it again."

"No, I can't. It was a once-in-a-lifetime love. The kind that makes your soul burn brightly."

Tristan rang off and Christos sank down in the leather executive chair, thinking of the tears in Ava's eyes last night, tears that made him believe that she, too, wanted that kind of once-in-a-lifetime happiness with him.

Ava wasn't sure what to expect when she got downstairs, but seeing her son playing with Ari wasn't it. Theo jumped off Ari's wheelchair when he saw her and ran to the open trunk of a Jaguar convertible, one of Christos's many cars. He'd given her the keys to a Rolls-Royce.

Theo grabbed a second water gun and brought it to her. She pushed her sunglasses up on top of her head. She hoped that Theo would suggest she be the bad guy. She certainly wouldn't mind dousing Ari with water.

"You can be the back-up detail."

"Thanks, sweetie," she said, dropping a kiss on Theo's head and accepting the weapon from him. "Where's your *baba*?"

"He had to take a call up at the main house," Ari said, giving her outfit the once over. "Are you sure that's what you should be wearing?"

She glanced down at her shorts and halter-style tank top. "We're going out on a boat."

"I know, but Christos may see some associates at the marina for lunch. You don't want to look like a tacky American."

She'd bought this outfit at Ann Taylor, the epitome of conservative American dress. She knew she didn't look tacky, but Ari made her want to defend her clothing. And she wasn't going to, because she'd learned the hard way that winning any argument with Ari was next to impossible.

"*Baba* isn't working today," Theo said.

"Business always comes first with Theakis men."

Ava smiled sweetly at the older man. "One of the things I've always liked about Christos is that he makes his own decisions."

"My son is stubborn, but also very loyal."

That was true. Christos's loyalty to Stavros had been one of the things that had driven the two of them apart. "He wants to be a good father to Theo."

"Mama, I think you need to stand behind that tree over there. The bad guys will be coming up from the garden."

She tossed her bag in the front seat of the convertible and got into position. Ari got to her as no one else could. She suspected it was partly because she didn't feel that she was good enough for Christos. Living here at the

Theakis compound brought home how different her life had been from Christos's.

"Mama?"

"Yes?"

"I hear someone coming."

She did, too. The footfalls were heavy on the stone walkway. She hoped it wasn't Antonio. The poor man had been doused with water a lot in the past week.

She heard the whirring of the motor on Ari's wheelchair and then Theo's small hand on her back. "When I give you the signal, we'll attack."

She nodded at her son. A shadow of a man was visible around the side of the large tree trunk and Theo nudged her with his elbow. She jumped out on one side while Theo covered their target from the other. They both fired at the same time, dousing not Antonio, but Christos.

"*Baba*, we got you!"

Christos grabbed his chest and staggered backward. Water dripped from his torso and face. Theo raced forward and pulled a piece of rope from his pocket. He took Christos's wrists in his hands.

"Mama, help me," he said.

Ava dropped her weapon and reached for Christos's wrists, which was when everything got a little crazy. Christos bent and picked up her gun with one hand and brought the other arm around her waist, holding her to his body. He held up the water gun to her face.

"Back away or the hostage gets it."

Theo put up his hands, still holding his gun and took

two steps back before he dropped into position and fired at Christos. Christos doused her with a shot of water to the face before turning his attention to Theo. Both of them raced down the path toward the garage and Ava stood there chuckling.

"I don't know what's gotten into him," Ari said.

"He's having fun."

"Fun has never been his problem."

"What *is* his problem?" she asked.

Ari shrugged and pulled a pair of sunglasses from his pocket. He turned the wheelchair toward the house and she realized that he was going to just roll away as if they weren't having a conversation.

"For someone who places so much emphasis on manners, you are very rude."

He stopped his chair and glanced over his shoulder at her. "Are you talking to me?"

"Do you see anyone else?"

"I don't like your American attitude."

She could name several things about Ari she didn't like. "I don't care for your Greek-male arrogance."

"Good."

He started back toward the house and she shook her head, watching him go. This was what she'd been trying to explain to Christos last night. The disdain that his father held for her made her days long and difficult. To his credit, Ari did seem to adore Theo and gave the boy a lot of attention.

She walked back toward the garage, noticing that

both Christos and Theo had disappeared. She had a feeling that she was going to get attacked guerilla-warfare style. And she needed that distraction, because she felt out of her element here. Something that Ari always induced in her.

She'd given birth to his grandchild, but apparently that wasn't enough for the older man to cut her any slack. She wondered if he knew the truth of what had happened in the past or just the tabloid version of everything that had transpired between her and Christos and Stavros. As observant as Ari was, she couldn't imagine he would have missed the fact that Stavros had been having an affair and that it wasn't with her.

She heard a rustling behind her a split second before she was hit in the back with an icy spray of water. She turned on her assailants, scooping her son up in her arms and wresting the squirt gun from him. She hit Christos in the face with the spray and then turned and ran for the car.

Theo's laughter filled the air and she felt something ease in her soul. No matter how much Ari might disapprove of her, this was exactly where she belonged. Christos captured them both, wrapping his arms around her from behind. She felt his warm body press against her. She tipped her head back on his shoulder.

"What did my father say to you?" he asked.

"Nothing important. Can you still take us out on your yacht?"

"Yes," he said. She could tell he wanted to ask her more questions, but she shook her head and set Theo down.

"Let's go!" Theo said, climbing into the car and fastening his seatbelt.

Christos tried to keep his mind on driving to the marina and off the wet shirt that clung to Ava's curves but it was hard...and that wasn't the only thing in that condition.

His mobile phone rang and he ignored it. He'd had it with his interfering father, friends and business associates. He needed this clear, bright, sunshiny day for himself and his family. Ava wrapped her arm around her waist and shivered a little as the breeze blew through the car. Keeping his eyes on the road, Christos reached behind him into the bag she'd stowed in the back seat and pulled out her sweater.

"Thanks," she said when he handed it to her. "Did you take care of all your business this morning?"

"Business?" he asked, wondering how she knew about it.

She shrugged. "Ari said you had a call. And last night you mentioned that there was a lot of stuff on your plate at work."

"Stuff? Is that what you think I do?" he teased. He didn't want to talk about business today or think about the heavy load he'd have to deal with tomorrow. Each day there was a new complication at the office. For just today, he wanted to feel...free. The way he used to when Stavros was still the one charged with carrying on the Theakis traditions.

"Meetings, conference calls, I don't know. What do you do?"

"Stuff," he said, unable to stop smiling over at her.

She playfully punched him in the arm. "You're in a good mood today."

"Am I not usually?" he asked, not wanting to assign too much significance to the fact that he was happy just to spend time with Theo and Ava. That wasn't like him. He didn't like to depend too heavily on someone else for his happiness. That was a road that led straight to disaster.

"Sometimes you are. You look very tense when you get home."

He turned into the parking lot at the marina and saw that Captain Platakis had his yacht ready to go. "Transition periods are always difficult in a business situation."

"In a personal one, too," Ava added.

"Indeed. Too bad that I can't map out a plan for our relationship the way I can for Theakis Shipping."

"Am I complicating your life?"

"In ways you can't even fathom."

"Oh, I think I can."

"What does *fathom* mean?" Theo asked from the back seat, reminding Christos that the boy was listening in on their conversation.

"Understand," Ava said.

"Oh. Why can't you understand?" Theo asked.

Christos reached around and ruffled the boy's hair. He

was way too young to have to learn that women had secrets a man could never unravel. "It's a man-woman thing."

"A love thing?"

Ava flushed. "Probably, sweetie. Are you ready to go out on the boat?"

"Wait a minute," Christos said, putting his hand on Ava's thigh to keep her from opening her door. He turned to Theo. "What's a love thing?"

"You know, *Baba,* when a man and a woman start to love each other."

Theo undid his seatbelt and climbed into the front seat, sitting on Ava's lap. She stroked her son's hair. "He asked a lot of questions about why you and I weren't together."

Christos wasn't sure what that meant. Did she think she had loved him?

He opened his door and climbed out of the car, needing distance. The happiness he'd felt earlier dimmed a little. What exactly was happening between him and Ava? Lust he could handle. Love…he didn't believe it existed. Sure, he cared for his father and Theo and couldn't even think of what he'd felt for Stavros. But love? Romantic love? He'd never experienced anything that made him believe it was real.

Not even with Ava.

"Christos?"

"Hmm?"

"Are you okay?"

"Sure. Why wouldn't I be?"

"You're glaring at the car."

"The sun's in my eyes," he said. "Theo, please run down to Captain Platakis and tell him we'll be ready in five minutes."

The boy hesitated and glanced at Ava. She stepped in front of him and turned toward Christos.

"He's afraid of water."

"What?"

She gave him a look that said she wasn't repeating it. He'd forgotten she'd mentioned that the boy didn't like water. "Theo, come here. Ava, will you go tell the captain we're here?"

She hesitated. And he gave her a hard look. He was to be Theo's father by marriage if not biologically, and that meant he had rights where the boy was concerned. Meant there were times when Ava was going to have to let go.

She sighed and he wondered a little more about the love thing she'd talked to Theo about. He was glad to have this very real problem to solve for his son. Fear of water he could help the boy get over. Understanding women…not so much.

Eight

Ava didn't feel comfortable on the platform in the middle of the room with Maria and the dress designer, Dorothea Festa, staring at her. She felt foolish standing there in a slip while they measured her and talked in Italian behind her back. Never had she felt more out of place than this moment.

Not even two days ago, when they'd returned from the boat trip to find that Christos's friends had arrived. Tristan and Guillermo had started bonding with her son, doing male things that had excluded her. But seeing Theo bloom under the male attention had soothed any jealousy she felt. Now she was in here, being fitted for a wedding dress worthy of a Theakis bride, while Theo was out near the pool with Tristan and Gui.

Christos was at the office, unable to take another day off even with his friends here. Her relationship with him had grown a little closer over the last few days, since their boat outing, but it was more the bond of parenting. Christos had backed her up against Ari when he had tried to have a nanny and private tutor brought in for Theo. He'd worked with Theo on basic Greek, and Theo had soaked up enough that he was now attending a day school in the village with other local children. Ava had volunteered to work in the classroom during the day. Her own rusty Greek was improving rapidly.

But their intimate relationship was at a standstill. She knew she was responsible for that by saying they shouldn't have sex until they were married. Or maybe Christos had just lost interest in her. He was busy at work and stayed out late at night with his friends. Perhaps she was assigning too much importance to herself and the impact she wished she had on him.

"Ms. Monroe, please hold your arms out."

Ava did as she was asked. The designer's assistant put the tape measure around her chest and then her waist and hips. She glanced down at her body dispassionately. She'd lost all the weight she'd put on when she'd been pregnant with Theo, but her body would never be the same.

Even the designer seemed to notice this as she patted that little bit of a belly Ava hadn't been able to get rid of.

"We can cover this with a full skirt," Dorothea said.

"I don't really want a full skirt," Ava said.

"I'll see what I can do. Will you be wearing a support garment underneath?" Dorothea asked.

"If I have to. Did you see the picture I cut out?" she asked.

"Yes. But that dress is too…common. I have some ideas that Mr. Theakis has approved."

"Christos shouldn't see the dress."

"Mr. Ari Theakis," Dorothea said turning back to Maria.

"Dorothea."

The woman glanced back at her. "Yes?"

"I'm not wearing anything that Ari suggested. If you don't think the dress I want is acceptable, I'm open to suggestions, but I will be making the final decision on the dress."

She bit her lower lip. "Of course, Ms. Monroe. Let me go get my design book. I'll be right back."

"Don't go to Ari," Ava said.

But Dorothea ignored her as she walked out of the room. Ava glanced at Maria, who refused to look over at her. She knew that the other woman wasn't going to side with her; she had her paycheck to think of. Dorthea's assistant busied herself with papers, perhaps writing down Ava's measurements.

Ava put on her robe and walked out of the second-floor sitting room where they were having the fitting. She wasn't sure what to do. Was she really going to let Ari intimidate her into wearing a dress she didn't want?

Someone cleared their throat behind her and she turned around. Guillermo. Gui. He was tall with a leonine mane of thick brown hair. His features weren't classically handsome but his face wasn't one you'd forget. He was tan with sunlines around his eyes and was a bit taller than Christos.

"Yes?"

"We're ready to have lunch and Theo wondered if you'd have time to join us."

She nodded. "Of course. Let me change and then I'll join you—on the terrace?"

"Yes," Gui said, but didn't leave. "Is everything okay?"

She shrugged, not wanting to lie to the man; she'd made a promise to Christos and to herself to stop pretending about things that made her uncomfortable.

"Do you want to talk about it? I have three sisters and two sisters-in-law…"

She laughed a little at the way he said it. One of his sisters-in-law was the Infanta of Spain—the royal princess and heir to the Spanish throne. "So you're used to listening to women's secrets?"

"Yes, I am. And if my sisters are to be believed I'm very good at helping with problems."

She was tempted. For the longest time she'd been on her own, handling her problems by herself. But she had no idea how to handle Ari. Standing up to him just made him more belligerent. Backing down made him gloat.

"Thanks for the offer, but this is something I think I should handle on my own."

Gui nodded. "If you change your mind, the offer is open."

"Thank you. I hope that Christos knows what a good friend you are."

"I remind him of it often," he said in that teasing way of his, but she was sure that he didn't have to.

The bond between the three men was closer than one between blood brothers. "How long have you known Christos?"

"Since we were ten."

"That long?"

"Yes. We met at school."

"Boarding school, right?"

Gui nodded. She took a deep breath, aware that she wasn't fooling him by talking about the past. She sat down on the loveseat under the window that looked over the sparkling blue water of the Aegean. "I don't know how to make Ari accept me."

Gui sat down next to her, putting his arm along the back of the loveseat. "Why would you want to?"

She looked into his diamond-hard eyes and tried to find the words to tell him how out of place she felt here on Mykonos and with Christos. But this strong, confident man would never be able to comprehend that, and she felt even less worthy of being a Theakis bride.

Christos wasn't having the best day. Two of the ships that they used to import goods from Asia were in quarantine and he couldn't find one official who would take a call from him to tell him what was going on. Hector, the man who was supposed to be in charge of these types of crises, was at the hospital with his wife, who was giving birth to their first child.

A text message from Theo had come in via Tristan's phone just minutes after he was told that he wouldn't be able to get an answer on the quarantine for another hour. So lunch with Theo and his friends was about the only thing he could do.

He pulled the Ferrari into the circle drive in front of the main house and got out. Antonio was waiting for him in the foyer with a drink and a look that said there was trouble brewing.

"Do I even want to know what's going on?"

"Probably not," Antonio said. "Your father is in conference with the designer he hired to make Ava's wedding dress. From what Maria told me, Ava wants a dress that is nothing like what your father ordered."

"Tell the designer to give Ava what she asked for."

"Your father is refusing to pay for it."

"I'll take care of it. In fact, let's get the old man out of the planning process. Please tell Ava that she is in charge of the wedding."

"Yes, sir."

"Where is she?"

"Upstairs. Master Theo is on the terrace with Tristan."

"Good. Tell them I'll join them in a few minutes."

"Yes, sir."

Antonio walked away and Christos went upstairs to

find Ava. The sitting room was empty so he went to her suite and knocked on the door. He heard the rumble of Gui's voice.

He wasn't going to jump to any conclusions. Yeah, right. What the hell was Gui doing in Ava's rooms?

Christos opened the door to the room and walked in as if he owned the place. Ava and Gui both stood up as he entered. He spared a hard glare for his friend and wrapped his arm around Ava's waist, pulling her into his body.

He took her mouth in a kiss that wasn't meant to be sweet or romantic. It was meant to stake a claim. But holding Ava in his arms always led him to one reaction.

God, he wanted her. He softened the kiss, sliding his hands down her back to her hips and wrapping one arm around her waist to anchor her to him.

The thin fabric of her robe wasn't much of a barrier.

"I'll be going now."

Christos took his time lifting his head, keeping one arm wrapped around Ava's waist. "What were you two discussing?"

"Your father," Gui said. "Women like to tell me their troubles."

"You always were a sucker for a damsel in distress."

"I'm not in distress. Thanks for listening," Ava said.

She pulled out of Christos's arms. "Are you home for lunch?"

"Yes. Theo invited me. Tristan put him up to it."

"I'll see you all downstairs in a few minutes," she said, walking out of the room.

They both watched her leave.

"I've never seen you so possessive before," Gui said.

Christos rubbed the back of his neck. He couldn't explain it to anyone, wasn't even going to try. He only knew that Ava was his and it was important that Gui and the rest of the world know it.

"What upset her?" he asked his friend.

"She's worried that you'll be embarrassed in front of society if the wedding isn't perfect."

Christos cursed under his breath. "I don't give a crap about that."

"I told her. But she's still concerned. Your father has her convinced that the Theakis set the style, not follow it."

"Ari couldn't care less about fashion," Christos said more to himself than Gui.

"He's making things difficult for Ava."

"Why?"

Gui shrugged. "Perhaps to make sure she'll stay. She did run away before."

"The paparazzi were all over her."

"I saw the coverage. That can be a lot to handle for a young woman."

"Yes," Christos said, not enlightening his friend that Ava had been driven away by more than the tabloids—Theakis Nanny Snags Both Brothers, one headline had screamed. His anger hadn't helped.

Gui walked toward the stairs. "Aren't you coming?"

"In a minute. I want to talk to Ava alone."

There had been nothing untoward between Gui and Ava when he'd walked in. Ava was reserved around his friends, and he was coming to realize that that was her way around most men.

This time he wasn't as caught up in the white-hot passion that blazed between them. It was still there, but he had more breathing room to make sensible decisions. Like branding her with his kiss? Yeah, well, he was still possessive where she was concerned.

Gui left and Christos looked around the sitting room while he waited for her. It wasn't sophisticated and cool the way his rooms were. She'd left her mark on the place. Pictures of Theo were mounted on the wall, along with little sayings that she was fond of. Nestled in one corner were the big story-time pillows and against the wall a rolling laptop caddy, which he knew she'd had brought in for Theo.

Ava was adjusting to living in his home just as she'd hoped she would.

When she exited her bedroom, Ava was surprised to find Christos waiting for her. He sat in the nest of pillows where she usually read Theo his bedtime story.

"Come here," he said.

She walked over and sat down next to him on the pillows. He drew her into his arms, gently rubbing his thumb over her lower lip.

Her mouth was a little swollen from the powerful kiss he'd given her. "I'm sorry if I hurt you."

"You didn't," she said. "It made me think I'd made a mistake asking you to wait until we were married…."

She didn't want to tell him how she'd stood in front of Maria and Dorothea and that snooty assistant and felt like the dirty little girl from the trailer park, someone who'd never be able to win his attention, much less keep it. That feeling harkened back to something that Stavros had said to her when he'd made a pass at her years ago: *Christos will never see you as anything more than some cheap American tail.*

Certainly Christos hadn't come after her when she'd left Mykonos and Greece to return to the States. But she'd always hoped that it had been anger and not a lack of caring that had made him let her go.

"Nothing was happening between Gui and myself. We were just talking."

"What about?"

"He was giving me advice about dealing with your father."

"Really? What did he suggest?"

She nibbled her lower lip. "Telling him to go to hell. But somehow I don't think I can do that."

Christos smiled at that. "I can't see you doing that either. I've left word with Antonio that you are in charge of our wedding. Don't let anyone bully you into anything."

"That's harder than it sounds. I'm not at all sure I can make the right choices."

"I'm sure you can. You're not the same young woman you were five years ago. Don't forget that."

"Does that mean you believe I've changed? That kiss you gave me when you came in…" Bringing it up might not be the wisest idea but nothing ventured, nothing gained. "It was a real claim-staking kind of kiss."

"Yes, it was."

"Nothing happened between Gui and myself," she said again.

"I know."

"You trust me?" she asked.

"I trust that nothing happened between the two of you." She swallowed hard, wanting to let it go.

"Because you trust your friend."

"What does it matter?"

"It matters to me."

"Why? We're here together. We are getting married."

That was exactly why it mattered so much to her. And she was so afraid that she was making Christos out to be this great love of her life in her mind. When the reality was…just another lie that she was telling herself.

"Because we *are* getting married."

He tucked her head closer to him, resting his chin on top of her head. "Ava, you are so complicated."

"So are you," she said. She had no idea what he really wanted from her.

"Why are you home?" she asked at last. She missed him during the day, although she was really trying to find a way to stand on her own. But right now she just closed her eyes and sank deeper into his arms.

"Theo asked me to come," he said, stroking her back.

"He misses you when you're gone."

"I miss him, too."

She tipped her head back and saw the sincerity in his obsidian eyes. "Even though you aren't sure he's your son."

"He's a Theakis and I do love him."

Though she'd wanted to hear him say that he believed Theo was his son, she didn't push. "I'm glad for that. I couldn't stay here if you didn't treat him right."

"Yet you'll stay here and let my father treat you poorly?"

"That's not fair. Your father is hard to deal with."

"I know. Do you want to live somewhere else?"

"What do you mean, not at the compound?"

He shrugged. "I've taken you away from the life you knew. I want this place to be your home."

Though it wasn't yet home, a physical place that she felt comfortable in, she didn't want to disrupt Theo's life with another move so soon. "I don't mind living here. Your father and I just have to sort things out. And I've talked to Theo's school about volunteering there. I think I can make this work...."

"Don't let him run you off," Christos said, and she had a feeling he was talking about way more than the wedding.

"I won't. I'm not going to let you do that to me, either."

"Good."

She smiled. "We'd better head down to lunch. Theo's probably already eaten but he'll expect to see you."

She tried to rise but he tugged her back into his arms.

"Yes?"

"I know you wouldn't betray me with Gui."

She caught her breath as the words sank in. Was he saying he trusted her? Or was this just an olive branch? A tentative offering that they could use to build a life together.

She leaned down and kissed him. She wanted to tell him with words all she felt about him, but words were something that Christos didn't trust from her. Actions, on the other hand, might be just what she needed to convince him that she was a woman worthy of being a Theakis bride.

Nine

His wedding day dawned cloudy and rainy. Not exactly a good omen, but then he'd never put much stock in things like fate. He controlled what happened around him with an iron fist and his own stubborn determination. Besides, the ceremony wasn't until dusk and after a lifetime of watching the seas he knew that the skies would clear long before the ceremony started.

Too bad women weren't easier to predict. Or, to be more specific, Ava. His focus had narrowed completely to her. His body was whacked out from wanting her so much. His emotions were a mess and he was caught somewhere between wanting to disappear into a job that could consume his life and walking away from being a Theakis to take Theo and Ava to some unnamed island.

He adjusted the tie at his throat, trying not to look at his reflection in the mirror. Ava had made a million and one small changes to her own life and he was well aware that he'd made none. He'd stood above her, superior in the knowledge that she'd betrayed him and should make amends. But now, coming to know her as he was, he suspected...

"Ready for the big day?" Tristan said, entering the room. He had a bottle of champagne in one hand and three glasses in the other. Gui was right behind him with a small digital camera.

"Ready as I'll ever be," Christos said. "I never thought I'd marry."

"It's not too late to change your mind," Guillermo said. Gui was a confirmed bachelor who'd even tried to talk Tristan out of marrying his long-time love, Cecile.

"Yes, it is," Tristan added. He put the glasses on the small table in the corner of the room and then opened the champagne. "You should know better than to suggest he could cancel, Gui. Ava would be devastated and I think that Ari would probably have a heart attack."

"Better never to get married than to have to end it later," Gui said. "You have to agree with that, Tris. Did you have doubts before you married Cecile?"

Tristan turned away and in his posture Christos saw the lingering pain of emptiness left by Cecile's death.

"No. I didn't have any doubts. I knew that she was the one woman for me."

Christos put his hand on his friend's shoulder and squeezed. He wished sometimes that his emotions were as powerful as Tristan's had been. But since Ava had come back into his life he'd been struggling to contain his emotions, working on not letting the possessiveness and jealousy that were always near the surface swamp him.

Gui raised one eyebrow at him. "What about you?"

He had no idea what he felt for Ava, only knew that she was his and he wanted the world to know it. "I'm not backing out. I've given my word."

"And the word of a Theakis is unbreakable," Theo said dancing into the room. He looked so cute in his tuxedo, like a Mini Me, Christos thought. Looking at the boy, he realized that this was his chance to make up for all the things he'd screwed up. With Theo he could make himself a better person.

"That's right, Theo."

"*Baba*, you look very handsome, just like Mama thought you would."

"How do you know that?"

"I heard her tell Maria."

Gui laughed. "You shouldn't eavesdrop, Theo. That's not polite."

"I didn't mean to."

Christos ruffled the boy's hair as Antonio entered the room carrying more champagne glasses. Antonio was dressed in a tuxedo and would also be serving as one of Christos's groomsmen.

"I think that this time it was okay," Christos said to Theo.

"I'm sure it was," Tristan said. "Let's have a toast to your *baba*, Theo."

Tristan poured champagne into each of the glasses. Ari entered in time to claim a glass. Seeing his formerly robust father in the wheelchair suddenly gave Christos pause. He struggled to see past the chair and most days was successful—the old man was so cantankerous that it was hard to pity him—but, today, when Stavros's absence was so palpable, it was harder.

Tristan made some kind of toast and Christos raised his glass and took a sip, but he couldn't stop looking at his father. He felt Theo's small hand in his grip and glanced down.

"I don't like this. Can I have something else to toast with?"

"It's not a proper toast if you don't do it with champagne," Tristan said. Being a Frenchman he had always believed that wine in all its forms was the only thing one should drink. "It's an acquired taste, Theo. All true gentleman enjoy it."

"It took me a while to get used to the taste as well."

"I will get some sparkling water for Theo." Antonio left the room.

"When did you get used to it, *Baba*?"

He shrugged. "Over time I think. Not being born French it may have taken me longer than Tristan."

"Touché," Tristan said with a mocking nod in his direction.

"Your father was born something better than French," Ari said.

"Greek?" Theo asked.

"No, a Theakis," Ari said. Christos met his father's gaze and for this one moment they were on the same page.

He glanced at Theo and wondered if he'd be happier knowing that the boy was really his son. The doubts were still there, but didn't change the way he felt for Theo. And today, he was happy to be a Theakis groom going to his bride. Happy to be the son of Ari. Happy that for once he and his father both wanted the same thing.

He pushed his doubts about Ava's past fidelity out of his mind, just for today.

Ava had never been one of those girls who'd had big dreams of her wedding day, mainly because she'd always known her father wouldn't pay for her to marry any man. But this was something out of a fantasy.

Once Christos had told her to take control of the wedding, she'd decided to do just that. She'd combed the society pages for wedding details so she'd have an idea of what the Theakis family were used to and then used her two weeks to plan an event that wouldn't embarrass them.

The end result was a ceremony and reception that she felt confident people would be talking about for a long time to come. But *she* still felt like a fraud. She felt as though the entire ceremony was one big lie. She put her head down in her hands.

"Don't do that, Ava, you'll smear your makeup," Laurette said. As promised, Christos had flown her and Paul in from Florida to help Ava prepare for the wedding, and Laurette was serving as her maid of honor.

"What am I doing?" she asked.

"Getting married to your very handsome Prince Charming," Sheri Donnelly said. Sheri worked for Tristan and had agreed to be in the wedding party as a favor to him. Guillermo's youngest sister, Augustina, was also serving as a bridesmaid. Augustina was sixteen and so beautiful that Ava had a hard time looking at her. She was also sweet and very shy.

"Prince Charming? Only if Prince Charming was arrogant and bossy," Ava said. Christos was definitely the only man for her, but she had to wonder sometimes why she'd fallen for such an opinionated man.

"There's no accounting for taste," Laurette said, fluffing her short blond hair. Laurette was the one woman in the world whom Ava actually felt comfortable with.

"Very funny," Ava said, finally smiling.

Sheri shook her head. "I'm in the same boat. In love with a guy I shouldn't be in love with."

"Tristan?" Ava asked. Though Sheri was dressed in a gown the same as the other bridesmaids' she still looked…well, plain. She blended into the background and was easy to ignore. But she was spunky, and Ava had noticed that the other woman was different when she was around Tristan.

Sheri flushed and looked away. "God, please tell me it isn't that obvious."

So glad to have someone else's problems to deal with instead of her own, Ava walked over to Sheri, putting her arm around the other woman's shoulders. "Only to someone in the same position."

"We're not in the same position. Christos is marrying you and he watches you with an intensity that makes it clear that he wants you."

"Wanting is not the same thing as loving. Christos is marrying me because…I don't know why he's marrying me. I think I'm making a horrible mistake."

Augustina left the mirror where she was fixing her lipstick. "Passion is never a mistake, Ava. That's how love starts."

"Who told you that?" Ava asked the younger woman.

She shrugged her delicate shoulder. "I'm Spanish. We know about passion."

She ruined her sophisticated moment by giggling after she said it. "Actually, Guillermo told me that."

"I can believe it," Ava said.

Augustina offered to help Sheri with her makeup and the two women moved to another corner of the room.

"Are you sure about this?" Laurette asked. "There's still time to call it off."

No, there wasn't. She wanted to marry Christos, had wanted to from the very first time she'd made love with him over five years ago. And though she'd never had any childhood dreams of a wedding, as soon as she'd held him in her arms, she'd had dreams of a marriage. Of having Christos as her husband.

"I'm not sure, but I can't call it off."

"Are you still worried about Theo?"

"No. Christos is a great father and I believe that if I said I couldn't stay here, he'd find a way to work something out between us. I'm not marrying him because I have to."

Laurette hugged her close. "Good. I like him. I think he's good for you."

"Ha, he's bossy."

"So are you. You need a man who will take care of you."

She wondered sometimes if that wasn't part of the appeal of Christos. He was so different from every other man she knew.

"It's almost time," Maria said, entering the room. She held a small wrapped box in one hand. Theo was behind her, looking adorable in his tux.

"Mama, I just had a champagne toast with *Baba* and I didn't like it."

"That's okay."

"The photographer is going to come in here in a minute to start taking photos," Maria said. "Theo, come over here and let me comb your hair." She turned to Ava. "This is for you."

She handed her the gift-wrapped box and then stepped away. Ava glanced down at the card, which simply stated her name in Christos's bold handwriting.

"I'll give you a minute to yourself," Laurette said, and joined Augustina and Sheri.

She unwrapped the box slowly. It was made of hardwood and inlaid with gold. The design on the top of the box was the Theakis family seal, something she'd seen many times over the last few weeks.

She opened the box and the fresh scent of cedar assailed her. She closed her eyes and breathed deeply. Then she opened them and looked inside. There was an embossed notecard. She lifted it out and read it quickly.

All Theakis are of the sea and here's something
to to remind you that now you are a Theakis, too.

She set the card aside and pulled out the velvet jeweler's bag beneath it. She loosened the tie at the top of the bag and pulled out the necklace inside. It was a beautiful diamond-and-sapphire encrusted choker with a platinum anchor dangling from it. There were matching earrings and a bracelet inside as well.

She caught her breath staring at them.

"*Baba* said these remind him of your eyes," Theo said, touching one of the sapphires.

She looked at her son and the women in the room and knew she was taking the right step. More than the jewels, Christos's words convinced her that, despite the fact that this wasn't her kind of wedding, she wasn't lying to herself. Marrying Christos was the right thing to do.

* * *

With the sun setting behind them, they repeated their vows on the terrace of the Theakis compound overlooking the Aegean Sea. Christos kissed Ava at the end of the ceremony with raw possessiveness, stamping his claim on her mouth to go along with the ring on her left hand that showed the world she was his.

Flashbulbs went off during the kiss and Christos felt a sense of impending doom. He'd invited several celebrity photographers, including one who would be doing a story on the wedding for one of the Sabina Group's magazines. But the public spotlight wasn't always kind, especially to Ava and him.

The flashbulbs brought back the anger he'd felt when the tabloids had broken the story of Ava's affair with Stavros.

He lifted his head and wrapped his arm around Ava's waist as they walked back down the aisle between their family and friends.

"Christos?"

"Hmm?"

"Why are you acting so…"

He glanced down at Ava. He couldn't begin to figure out what he felt, but he knew *happy* was too tame a word for it. He banished the thought of the past as he looked at her. Knew the only way he was going to find any semblance of peace was to stay focused on Ava and Theo and the future he was slowly carving out for himself.

He arched one eyebrow at her. "So…?"

"Possessive, I guess. I'm yours now," she said.

There was a note in her voice that he couldn't place and he didn't try. "About damn time."

"Do you mean that?"

"*Moro mou*, I'm not indecisive about anything especially if it involves you or Theo."

She hugged him tightly to her, standing on tiptoe and kissing him. "This is one of the happiest days of my life. I can't believe we're married."

"Well, believe it. You are my wife."

She blinked back tears, then rubbed her nose and tried to turn away. "Oh no. My makeup is going to be ruined."

Christos had no idea how to stop her tears. Didn't understand where she'd gone in her head to start crying, so he did the only thing he could think of. He took her face in his hands and kissed her. Not with the raw masculinity that he'd used to brand her in front of his friends and family earlier. But with all the pent-up and unrevealed emotions that were coursing through him.

She clung to his shoulders, holding on to him, and he realized this was what he wanted. Like the symbol on the necklace he'd given her, he wanted to be her anchor when the seas of life got stormy and she didn't have anything or anyone else to cling to.

He lifted his mouth. Her eye makeup was safe, but her lipstick was completely obliterated. Her lips were soft and pink from his kisses, slightly swollen, and he couldn't wait to get to their room.

She touched her fingers to her lips. He stared down

into her eyes, let his gaze drift lower over the long length of her neck to the choker he'd given her. It looked perfect there. He skimmed his finger around her neck, tracing the seam where skin met diamonds and sapphires. He ended with a touch of the silvery anchor.

"You have the prettiest eyes I've ever seen," he said. "They remind me of the sea." The truth was, he lost a little bit of himself each time he looked into her eyes. They were wide and held depths that he was only beginning to realize she had. This time around, their relationship was so much stronger, he thought. And though he'd never admit it to a soul, he thought that Ava had been very wise to insist they not sleep together until they were married.

She flushed a little. "I like your eyes, too."

"We're married now," he said as their bridal party joined them on the steps of the main house.

He noticed that Tristan and Sheri were standing off to one side. Tristan's body language wasn't all that hard to read as he leaned over his surprisingly interesting secretary. He was definitely attracted to her. Sheri said something and Tristan's laughter echoed in the air. Christos couldn't remember the last time he'd seen Tristan that relaxed with a woman.

"Yes, we are."

He hugged her close as a photographer bustled around arranging the group for the shot. Christos brushed his lips over Ava's ear. "I can't wait for our wedding night."

She swiveled her hips against his and then reached

up with one hand, wrapping it around his neck, drawing his head forward. She kissed him with the same possessiveness he'd shown earlier in front of their wedding guests. "Me, neither."

Tristan clapped him on the back. "Congratulations, Mr. and Mrs. Theakis! Are you sure you know what you are getting into, Ava?"

"Yes, Tristan, I'm sure. Christos is the man I've always dreamed of marrying."

Ava was drawn away by the women to fix her makeup before the photographer started taking more pictures, and her words lingered.

"A woman's dreams are fragile things," Tristan said.

So were a man's, if the ghosts in Tristan's eyes were any indication. "Are you all right?"

"Fine. I'm happy for you. You've been alone too long."

"I've never been alone," Christos said. He'd made it a point to ensure he always had a lovely woman on his arm or in his life.

"My mistake. I like Ava."

"I do, too," Gui said, coming up behind them. "And this little monkey."

Gui lifted Theo up on his shoulder and Christos felt blessed for the first time ever, not only by the friends he had in his life but by being a Theakis. With Theo by his side, he didn't feel that he was second best, and when he glanced down and saw his father smiling while he chatted with one of the Theakis relatives, he realized that he felt almost at peace.

He scowled. He didn't trust the feeling and from the past knew it couldn't last. Not for the first time, he resented the fact that he had to plan for a future that was as stormy as the seas during a hurricane. But at the same time, his reality was that, whenever he got this feeling of rightness…something bad was waiting around the corner.

"Christos?" Gui had been watching his friend's expression.

"Yes?"

"You okay, man?"

"I've fulfilled my destiny as a Theakis. Of course I'm okay."

Gui gave him an odd look, but Christos turned away and chatted with some business associates, faking an enthusiasm he no longer felt.

Ten

"Oh, Christos, this is so romantic. I didn't think you'd do anything like this."

Christos hadn't thought he would, either, but Tristan's comment that morning about how women dreamed of their wedding day had made him think about their wedding night and making it into a romantic fantasy. It had taken less than twenty minutes on the phone to get everything as he wished it to be.

"After all the trouble you went through planning our wedding, it was the least I could do."

He set Ava on her feet in the luxurious suite that he'd rented for the night. They'd leave in the morning for Paris for their two-week honeymoon. But tonight they were in Athens at one of the five-star properties his family owned. The owner's suite was large, with the best marble flooring imported from Italy, priceless works of art adorning the walls and Louis XIV furniture. Beautiful, opulent, yet it all paled compared to the woman in his arms.

She danced around the room, her strawberry-blond hair fanning out around her. There was a restless energy about her that underscored the fact that, even though he could hold her in his arms, he never really understood her.

"You're staring at me," she said, coming to a stop in front of the balcony doors.

"I know."

"Usually I'm the one who does the staring," she quipped.

"You're effervescent tonight. I can't seem to stop looking at you."

The lighting in the room was dim and candles flickered on all the surfaces. Pale-pink rose petals made a trail on the floor to the bedroom.

"Am I?" She tipped her head to the side, giving him a seductive look from under her eyelids.

He nodded. "I've been waiting for this moment since I came back into your life."

"I've been waiting for this moment since you left my life. I can't believe today has been real."

"Come over here and I'll prove it."

She smiled over at him in a dreamy way that he thought meant she might be a little buzzed from the champagne she'd drunk at their reception. She'd danced with Theo and with him, but no one else. It was as if she were sending him a direct signal that she was his.

"*Moro mou*, come here."

She shook her head. "Not yet."

"Why not?"

"You'll kiss me and I'll forget that I want this night to last forever."

"I promise it'll last forever," he said, wondering if that was the truth. His erection strained against his zipper now that they were alone and he knew that he was going to have her. At last. Well, if the first time didn't last forever, he'd make it up to her the second time he took her. He didn't plan on sleeping much tonight anyway.

She didn't say anything but kicked off her high heels and walked toward him in that sexy dress she'd changed into before they'd left the reception. The skirt danced around her legs and she put an extra swivel in her hips.

"Ava…"

"Christos…."

"Stop teasing me."

"Is that what I'm doing?"

"You know you are."

"Why don't you stop me?"

"Because you don't want me to," he said.

She stopped. "You're right, I don't. I want to tease you until you can't sit there and beckon me. Until that passion you do such a good job of hiding forces you to come to me—"

He lunged for her, pulling her tight to his body. Holding her by her hips as his mouth found hers. He plundered her lips, pushing his tongue deep into the cavern of her mouth, swallowing her gasp and tasting that champagne he knew she was buzzing from.

He didn't lift his head until she was clinging to him. "Like that?"

"Just like that. I've missed being in your arms," she said, curling herself around him.

He lifted her into his arms again, carrying her over the rose-petal path to the bedroom. She kept one hand at the back of his neck, her long fingers toying with the hair there. Every nerve-ending in his body was focused on one thing, one purpose. And each brush of her hands against him aroused him more.

He set her on the bed in the middle of the rose petals and stepped back. He reached for the dimmer switch on the wall, turning it so a low, ambient light filled the chamber.

He kicked off his shoes, toed off his socks and shed his jacket, tossing it toward the padded chair in the corner of the room.

He wanted this to be a slow seduction, their first time together in so long, but he couldn't stop his body. It was as if a red haze had come over him and all he could see was Ava and her soft curves.

All he wanted was to feel her naked skin against his and the welcoming warmth of her body wrapped around him. He wanted to plunge deep inside her and take her until time dropped away. Until there was nothing but the two of them and the kind of passion he'd never found with anyone else.

"Christos, are you coming to bed?'

"In a minute." Hell, he didn't think a minute was going to be enough time to bring him down. All he could smell each time he breathed was her perfume. All he could taste lingering in his mouth was her. All he could see was Ava.

He told himself to take it slow but slow wasn't in his programming with this woman. She was pure feminine temptation and he had her in his arms. He stepped purposefully toward her.

She sat up. "Wait! I forgot I have something special to wear tonight."

"The choker I gave you earlier would be fine but anything else is a waste of time."

"Please, Christos. It'll just take a second."

He nodded. He could deny her nothing tonight; she was so radiant.

"I left word for our bags to be unpacked."

"I can find what I want to wear. Will you wait for me out there?"

He complied and then paced the outer room until she called him back.

She was wearing some silky thing that made her so desirable he barely noted what it was.

He crossed the room and took her face in his hands, staring down at her and then lowering his mouth. He tried to harness his passion this time so he didn't over-whelm her. But the need that had been riding him since—hell, since he'd seen her at that boarding school in Florida—slipped out of his control.

His hips thrust against her as his hands slid down her back, finding the hem of the nightdress and pulling it up until he could caress her soft skin. Her thighs were firm and smooth and, as he caressed his way higher, he encountered only the smooth flesh of her buttocks.

He groaned deep in his throat, running his finger along the curves of her flesh, exploring her thoroughly. She said his name, a breathless gasp that told him she was right there with him. And then he traced his way between her legs.

"Christos…"

His name falling from her lips was exactly what he wanted to hear. "Loosen your top, Ava. Bare your breasts for me."

She shivered in his arms. Her mouth found his and kissed him just as deeply as he had her a moment earlier. When she drew back she took his bottom lip between her teeth and nipped at it.

Her hands went behind her back to the tie that held the bit of silk up. The movement thrust her chest forward. His eyes narrowed as the fabric slowly parted from her body, slipping away from her skin. "Are you sure this is what you want?" she asked, teasing him now.

He left off caressing her and caught her wrists in one of his hands, holding them behind her back.

He lowered his head and pushed the fabric fully down from her chest with his other hand. And then he stared down at her breasts, creamy and full, their tips hard and straining. He couldn't resist the invitation to take one nipple in his mouth, suckling at her. Her legs moved restlessly, one of them coming up to wrap around his hips.

He released her wrists and ran one fingertip around her aroused flesh. She trembled in his arms. Her fingers drifted down his back and then slid around front to work on the buttons of his shirt. But he was too impatient to wait for that. He set her on her feet and ripped his shirt open.

He growled deep in his throat when she leaned forward to brush kisses against his chest. She bit and nibbled, bringing him to the brink. No way could he wait another second.

He pulled her to him and lifted her slightly so that her nipples brushed his chest. Holding her carefully he rotated his shoulders and rubbed against her. Blood roared in his ears. He was so hard, so full right now that he needed to be inside of her body. The skirt of her nightgown bunched between their bodies and he shoved it out of his way.

He caressed her smooth thighs. She was so soft. She moaned as he neared her center and then sighed when he brushed his fingertips there.

He slipped one finger into her and hesitated for a second, looking down into her eyes.

She bit down on her lower lip and he felt the minute movements of her hips as she tried to move his touch to where she needed it.

He was beyond teasing her or prolonging anything. He needed her now. He carried her to the bed and fell on it, bringing her down on top of him before rolling over so she was beneath him.

He looked down into her face. Her eyes were closed for a second as she shifted her hips and rubbed herself against him.

"Hurry, Christos."

He didn't need her to ask twice. Reaching between their bodies he freed himself and covered her with his body. Their naked loins pressed together and he shook under the impact.

Now. He adjusted his hips, positioning himself, and then entered her with one long, hard stroke.

She moaned his name and her head fell back, leaving the curve of her neck open and vulnerable to him. He bit softly at her neck and felt the reaction all the way to his toes when she squirmed in his arms and thrust her hips back toward him.

A tingling started in the base of his spine and he knew his climax was close. But he wasn't going without Ava. He wanted her with him.

She moved more frantically in his arms and he moved deeper inside her with each stroke. Breathing out through his mouth, he tried to hold back the inevitable. He slid one hand down her abdomen, through the slick folds of her sex, finding her center. He stroked the aroused flesh with an up and down movement, circled with his forefinger then scraped it very carefully.

Then he penetrated her as deeply as he could. She cried out his name.

"Look at me, Ava. Open your eyes."

She did, and in that instant, as everything in his body tightened and he started to climax, he wanted to love her. Wished there was a way he could forgive the past, because he knew he held the future in his arms.

Christos rolled over in the middle of the night and felt the warmth of Ava's body. They'd made love once more before falling asleep, and he'd carefully stripped the silk slip from her body and taken the time with her he'd wanted to the first time.

He'd opened the drapes to let the light of the moon into the room, and the balcony doors so that a cool night breeze stirred the air around them. Goosebumps were visible on Ava's naked skin. He traced his finger down the line of her body.

He came to the small bump of a belly left from her pregnancy, the small trace that Theo had left on her body. The trace of a child who was at the root of their marriage—and at the root of his distrust of her. He knew he had to do something about that.

He'd tried hard over the past few weeks to allow himself to see the woman that was Ava. And to be honest, he didn't believe the woman she was today would cheat on him. But that girl in the past…he wasn't as sure about her.

She stirred in his arms, rolling onto her back. He propped himself up on one elbow and continued to caress her, finding the tiny stretch marks left by her pregnancy, and everything within him solidified. He wanted to mark every part of Ava as his own. He wanted to plant his seed in her womb. He wanted to watch her grow heavy with his child and then be there from the first breath that child took.

It didn't change the way he felt about Theo…that boy was his now, and nothing on earth could change that.

"Christos?"

"Hmmm?"

She touched his face with soft fingers and he realized that she always did that. "What's the matter?"

"Nothing."

"I wish…I wish I were the slender girl I was the first time."

"I don't."

She tilted her head. He continued tracing over the stretch marks left by her pregnancy. "Did you like carrying the Theakis heir?"

"You mean your son?" she asked.

He shrugged. "Did pregnancy agree with you?"

She looked as if she were going to pursue the topic but then stopped. "Yes. I had morning sickness at the beginning but then…yes, it was very pleasant."

He didn't ask her any more questions, lowering his head to trace the lines with his tongue. Her hands fell to his head, caressing his scalp with her fingers.

"You know what I liked best about it?" she asked in a soft tone.

"What?" He lifted his head looking up the length of her naked body to meet her sea-blue eyes.

"That I wasn't alone anymore," she said, then glanced away as if she'd said too much.

He slid up over her. Her legs parted for him so that he rested in the cradle of her body. "Would you like another child, *moro mou*?"

With his erection at the portal of her body, he knew this wasn't the time for a discussion about their family and their future. But before he drove into her and made her his again, he needed to know.

She put her hands on his chest, holding him back from entering her body.

"Would you?"

"Yes," he said, bending down to capture the tip of her breast in his mouth. He sucked her deep inside, his teeth lightly scraping against her sensitive flesh. His other hand caressed at her other breast, arousing her, making her arch against him in need.

"Should I get birth control this time?" he asked her. "Or do you want to try for another child?"

Her gaze met his. "Yes, I think I would."

She reached between them and took his erection in her hand, bringing him closer to her. "I need you now."

He lifted his head and watched her as he slid deep into her body.

She started to close her eyes as he made love to her. "Keep your eyes on mine, Ava."

He thrust slowly in and out of her body, building them both toward climax with deliberation. He stared into her eyes, wanting to see—needing to know—how susceptible she was to him. There was no room for lies in their bed and when they were close like this he believed everything about Ava.

She slid her hands down his back, cupping his buttocks as he thrust deeper into her. Staring deep into her eyes made him feel as though their souls were meeting. She started to tighten around him, climaxing before him. He gripped her hips, holding her down and thrusting into her again before he came with a roar of her name. He held her afterwards.

Ava ran her hands slowly up and down his back. He heard her breath catch and then felt the warmth of her tears on the side of his face. Propping himself up on his elbows he stared down at her and wiped the tears away with one thumb.

"What's the matter?"

She swallowed and then glanced down at his chest, at the gold medallion that swung free from his body. She caught it, tracing her finger over the pattern of the Theakis family crest.

"Ava? Tell me, *moro mou*," he said.

"I'm just so happy. I never thought you'd forgive me and we'd have this."

He bent his head and kissed her so she wouldn't be able to see the doubt that still lingered in his heart about

Theo. He wanted the peace he felt to be real and knew there was only way to make that happen.

He was going to have to have the boy tested.

Eleven

Ava rested her head on Christos's chest, listening to the solid beating of his heart. Wrapped in his arms, it was easy to pretend that the problems they'd had in the past were gone. Easy to pretend that Christos believed her about Theo and that she no longer had to prove herself to him because of the problems that Stavros and Nikki had left behind.

She tried never to think ill of them, but their marital problems were like a disease that had spread out to affect her and Christos, not just in the past, but now.

She'd come to understand a new truth about herself when she'd had Theo. And these past few weeks on Mykonos, she had learned to understand Christos so much better now than she ever could have before. And because she had her own weaknesses, she didn't want him to feel that way with her. That she was *his* weakness. Christos had given her something she wasn't sure she could have found on her own.

"Are you sleeping?" he asked.

She felt the vibration of his words in his chest and under her ear. She shifted in his embrace, tipping her head so she could see the underside of his jaw.

"No. Too much to think about." This had been at once the most terrifying and exciting day of her life. She felt that, if she went to sleep, she might wake up and find none of it had happened. That she was still a single mother living with Theo in Florida.

She tugged on his chest hair in retaliation. "Were you serious about wanting more children?"

"Yes."

"I'm glad. I think Theo will benefit from having another sibling."

"Yes, he will. Plus I think it will make our family more solid."

"Solid is no guarantee of happiness—or safety. Look at what happened to Stavros and Nikki. Who would look after Theo if something happened to us?"

He rubbed his hand up and down her arm. "Nothing's going to happen to us, but in such a case I've asked Tristan to be Theo's guardian."

"Shouldn't you have discussed this with me first?" She liked Tristan, but she wasn't sure he was parent material. He was more like the crazy fun uncle than a responsible guardian. As much as she didn't like Ari, she thought he might be a better choice.

"I made the decision before I left for Florida to pick up Theo."

"Oh," she said not really sure how to take that. "What about your father?"

"My *patera* isn't strong enough to contend with a young man. Tristan is the best choice."

"What if you're wrong?" she asked. Her heart ached at the thought that something could happen to her and Christos and Theo would be left alone in the world.

"I'm not."

"I hate when you do that." His confidence was part of what attracted her to him, but she wished at times he'd at least acknowledge that he was human and was as fallible as everyone else.

"I know. I'm sorry I didn't consult you, but there wasn't time. Would you like to ask your friend Laurette to be a co-guardian? I think that Theo will need a female influence."

"She's actually his godmother from when I had him baptized. And I do like Tristan."

"Good."

"So, having another child…"

"Yes?"

"Does this mean you finally believe me about Theo?"

She held her breath, unable to believe she'd finally had the courage to ask him that question again. He closed his eyes, rolled over so that she was under him. Her legs parted and he settled against her. His arms braced on either side of her body. He brought his mouth down hard on hers.

When he came up for air long minutes later, his hands moved over her body with intent. She was tempted to let him distract her and be swept away by the passion that flowed so easily between them. But she had to know. In a way, she already had started to believe they were going to have a real marriage, yet they couldn't unless there was real trust between them.

She pulled back, putting her hands on his face and holding him still. She stared up into his obsidian eyes that were so like the son's he hadn't acknowledged he believed was his. Sure, to Theo and the world he'd claimed her son, but she knew he had doubts. Had she shown him enough of who she really was to change his mind about her?

"Please answer me," she said at last.

"Theo is our son."

She believed him. Christos wasn't the kind of man to say things lightly. She wondered if she should ask him how he felt about her. If he thought he could ever love her. But those words weren't easy to find and she was much too scared that she might find out that he couldn't love her to ever say them aloud.

Instead she lifted her hips toward his and felt him slip inside her body. Their eyes met and held again and he took her with carefully measured thrusts until they both climaxed at the same time. She felt the warm spill of his seed deep inside her body and she wondered if giving him another child would make him love her.

But she knew that she'd done all she could. She'd just have to fill their house and relationship with love. Christos was a smart man and more intuitive than he let on. Instinctively she knew she hadn't made a mistake in marrying him.

Paris was vibrant and romantic and Ava soaked it up. They'd had dinner with Tristan's family last night and today Christos was escorting his new bride around the city to fashionable boutiques recommended by Tristan's sisters.

His mobile rang and he glanced at the caller ID before answering.

"Yes, Antonio?"

"Sorry to disturb you, sir, but Master Theo wanted to talk to you."

"No problem, put him on."

"Baba?"

"Yes, Theo?" He missed the little boy and had stopped thinking of Theo as the Theakis heir. How had that happened? When had he gone from thinking of Theo as his nephew to thinking of the boy as his son? It was as if the relationship and his distrust of Ava had nothing to do with Theo. He knew that made no sense. "How was the allergy testing today?"

"Okay, my back hurts and is very itchy."

"That will go away in a few hours. I'll have Antonio put some salve on it."

The little boy talked about other things, games he'd played with his grandfather, and Christos had a new sense of peace about the relationship. He'd asked the doctor to take a cheek swab for a DNA test from the boy while he was conducting the allergy test. He imagined he'd soon have the answers he needed to move forward in his relationship with Ava.

And he needed to know if he or Stavros was the father for insurance purposes anyway.

He wanted to believe Ava, but a part of him, that long-cynical part, was refusing to without proof.

"When are you coming home?" Theo said, a note of something in his voice.

"Not for five more days. Is something wrong?"

"I'm having trouble breathing," Theo whispered, probably so that Antonio wouldn't hear him.

"Ask Antonio for your inhaler," Christos said.

"It's in the room with Uncle Gui. I don't want…"

"Theo, it's not a weakness. Gui has seen me wheezing and using an inhaler many times. Remember when I had to use it on the yacht?"

"Yes."

"Go now," Christos said, using a firm and authoritative voice that he hoped his son would obey.

"I…"

"No arguments, Theo. Do it."

"Yes, sir." Then Theo heard him calling for Antonio.

Before his butler came back on the line, Ava emerged from the dressing room wearing a slim-fitting black gown that plunged between her breasts and had a slit up one leg. "How do I look?"

"Wonderful. You are definitely getting that one."

"Is everything okay?" she asked, indicating the phone in his hand.

"Theo was having a bit of breathing trouble and didn't want to use the inhaler in front of Gui."

"Let me talk to him," Ava said, holding out her hand.

"He's gone already. I'm waiting for Antonio. I've got it under control. Go try on another dress."

"I want to speak to my son," she said.

"Is he not *our* son?"

"Yes, he is. I'm sorry. I just have a hard time letting go."

"You don't have to let go. We're partners now," he said. As he spoke he realized how much he wanted those words to be true. The only way that was going to happen was if he started trusting Ava. Truly trusting her. And trusting her meant not relying on a paternity test.

He'd tell the company lawyers that they'd have to find a way to insure Theo without the test. The boy was clearly a Theakis.

He looked into those beautiful sea-blue eyes of hers and realized the truth that he had been running from. That he was lost without this woman. And if she left him again…betrayed him again…he'd never recover.

"Christos?"

"Hmm?"

"Are you okay?"

"Yes."

"Let me put my own clothes back on and we can leave."

He nodded and kept listening on the open phone line until Antonio came on. "Theo's fine now. Would you like me to have the doctor come back and monitor him for the evening?"

"Yes, and then direct him to call my mobile, Antonio."

"Yes, sir," Antonio said.

There was a note in his voice that Christos couldn't place. "What?"

"Your father has hired a nanny for Theo. Master Theo doesn't understand why she's here."

"Thanks, Antonio, for the information. I'll take care of this with my father."

"I figured you would."

He hung up the phone just as Ava came out of the dressing room. She had none of the clothes in her hands that she'd been trying on. "Where are your dresses?"

"I don't want anything here."

"Ava?"

"I want to go home. I'm enjoying the city and being alone with you, but I miss Theo."

Christos drew her into his arms and gave her a quick kiss on the cheek. He missed Theo, too, and he had plenty of pressing business to attend to.

"I'll call the pilot and have him ready the plane. Do you want to leave now?"

"You don't mind?"

He shook his head. "I want you to be happy, Ava."

She smiled up at him, that brilliant smile that made his breath catch in his chest. He couldn't resist kissing her. Running his hands down her back and pulling her firmly into his arms. She was his. His. He'd never had anything that wasn't given to him because of the circumstances of his birth—aside from Ava and Theo.

"Having your trust has given me a joy that I can't explain." Her optimism made him wonder if he should explain right now about the paternity test. But he didn't want to dim it. Hell, who was he kidding? He knew that she'd be angry and disappointed if she learned what he'd done and he wanted more time to enjoy the peace that had grown between them during their honeymoon.

Christos barely had the car turned off when Theo bolted from the house and down the steps. Ava opened her door and stepped out of the car just as Theo reached her. He jumped up and she caught him in her arms, hugging his small body close to hers. Tears burned her eyes as she held him close. The time spent away from her son had just felt like too long.

Christos came up and Theo immediately wriggled in her arms, trying to get to his father. She handed him to Christos and watched the two embrace. Her life felt complete, so perfect and happy that she almost was afraid to believe it was real.

How had she gotten all of this? She'd been living her single life, so sure that she'd never find a happy ending with Christos, yet here it was. The pot of gold at the end of the rainbow she'd thought she'd never see again.

Christos glanced at her, catching her staring yet again. He gave her one of those long level looks of his and she shrugged.

"I like seeing my guys together."

Theo had an arm slung around Christos's shoulder as he walked over to her. "We like seeing you, too, right, Theo?"

"That's right."

"We have a surprise for you," Ava said.

Actually they had all kinds of surprises for Theo. Ava had bought him a stuffed bear in a shop in Paris and Christos had gone wild in another toy store, buying all kinds of things.

"What is it?" Theo asked, jumping from foot-to-foot when Christos put him down.

"I'm not sure we should give it to him," Christos said, looking very intent and serious.

Ava hid a smile behind her hand, enjoying her son and his father. Just enjoying everything that this moment was bringing her.

"Please, *Baba*."

"Were you a good boy?" Christos asked.

The two of them joked around as Christos carried Theo up to the house. Ava paused there on the circle drive of the large, luxurious house and for a minute flashed back to the small, single-wide mobile home she'd grown up in. When she'd met Christos, she'd been pretending her past didn't exist and had built a world based on lies. But now she saw that some of the things she'd told herself weren't lies. Christos *was* a good man. The kind of man she could safely give her heart to.

She loved him. Heck, she'd always loved him, and acknowledged to herself that she'd never stopped. But now that love felt bigger, more encompassing than it had before, because this time she wasn't his secret lover.

She glanced down at her left hand and the large platinum and diamond band there. She was his wife.

She'd just caught up to them near the entrance of the house when Ari's Bentley pulled up.

"I need to talk to you privately, Christos," Ari said through the car's open window.

"Can it wait?"

Ava guessed his father wanted to talk about Christos's dismissal of the nanny Ari had hired. He'd told her about that on the way home.

"No."

Christos handed her the bag with Theo's gifts in it. "Why don't you go inside with Theo and show him his surprises?"

"Yes, I will."

Christos brushed a light kiss against her lips and then nudged her toward the stairs with a discreet push on her backside. Theo held her hand as they entered the house.

"What did you get me?"

She smiled at the eagerness in his voice and drew him into one of the open rooms on the first floor.

There were three long couches and some armchairs in the room.

She sat down on one of the couches and slowly opened the bag, drawing out one of the gifts. "First you have to tell me one new thing you did while I was gone."

He climbed up on the couch next to her and put the present in his lap. "I went on a speedboat ride with Uncle Gui."

"Was it fun?" she asked, hearing the enthusiasm in Theo's voice. He liked having so many men in his life, and their love of boats seemed to be conquering Theo's fear of water.

Theo's eyes sparkled. "Yes, it was. We went so fast nothing could catch us. Can I open this now?"

She nodded and he tore the wrapping off the gift box. He opened the lid and pulled out the stuffed bear she'd chosen for him.

"Thank you, Mama," he said, hugging the bear to his chest and leaning over to give her a kiss.

"What are you going to call him?"

"Hmm…Fluffy."

"Fluffy it is. Are you ready for another present?"

He nodded. She drew out another package and handed it to him. "Tell me something else you did while I was gone."

He took the long box and held it with two hands. She could tell his attention wasn't on the question she asked but on trying to figure out what was in the box. She knew he was going to love this present. It was Spy Gear.

The play set contained everything Theo would need when he pretended to be a bodyguard.

"Theo?"

"Yes, Mama?"

"Tell me something so you can open this one."

He ran his fingers over the colorful pattern on the wrapping paper. "The doctor did a test on me."

"For allergies?" she asked. "Did they prick your back?"

"Yes and he put something in my mouth and rubbed it on my cheek."

"What? Why did he do that?" she asked.

Theo shrugged. "I don't know. Can I open my present?"

"Yes," Christos said coming into the room.

"What other kind of test did the doctor perform?" she asked.

Christos rubbed the back of his neck and looked away from her and she knew the answer before he said it.

"A paternity test."

She stared at Christos, unable to really understand what he'd said. "I thought you and I had already come to an understanding on this topic." Her ears were buzzing.

"We have," he said.

"They why did you have a test done?"

"Mama, don't get mad. The test didn't hurt me."

She hugged Theo to her side and bent to give him a kiss. Christos had gone behind her back.

This was the second time she'd allowed Christos Theakis to break her heart. When was she going to learn that he couldn't be trusted?

Twelve

"It's okay, sweetie. I...I just thought your father and I had an understanding."

"What's an understanding?" Theo asked.

Ava's eyes never left her son's. And Christos saw her shrinking away from him as the seconds passed. He'd ordered the test so he could give her what she wanted, bring real trust to their relationship. And he'd decided that he wasn't going to hear the results.

But now he felt as though he shouldn't even have made the gesture. He saw the hurt and anger in her. And understood it on one level, but on another...well, he wasn't the type of man to trust blindly and she had to have known that.

"An agreement. Like the one you and I have where

you always tell me the truth no matter what," Ava said, finally lifting her gaze.

Theo put the box on the couch and stood up, looking up at him with a serious expression that he knew mirrored his own. "Did you lie, *Baba*?"

How to answer this? "No, Theo, I didn't."

"Did I misunderstand you when you said that you trusted me?" Ava asked.

He shook his head. This conversation was complicated and delicate. Not fit for the ears of their four-year-old son. He swept the boy up in his arms and hugged him so tightly that Theo squirmed. *His son.*

"Will you give your mother and I some privacy?"

"Yes," Theo said. Christos put him down and Theo ran out of the room, taking the stuffed bear with him.

Ava had her arms wrapped around her waist and was staring at him in a way she never had before, as if the wind had been knocked out of her. Even that day at the school when he'd come back into her life, she hadn't looked like this.

"Ava—"

"Don't try to sugarcoat this or explain your actions. I made it clear that I needed your trust on this issue, Christos."

"I know that. I do trust you."

"Yeah, right."

"Don't be sarcastic. You can't carry it off."

Her arms dropped to her side. "I'll be whatever I like. I'm the injured party here."

He shook his head at her. "Put yourself in *my* shoes, Ava. I saw you and Stavros together. Nikki knew he was sleeping with another woman that summer and you were the only one near him."

Those were images he'd never been able to get out of his head. Though they were fading with time.

"Put yourself in my shoes, Christos…you give your virginity to a man you think you love and your boss comes on to you and you end up losing the man you love, your job and your family."

"I'm sorry that your family didn't stand by you," he said, unable to fathom her family abandoning her, because his never would. Even when he was at his wildest his father had still kept in touch. And he'd always had Guillermo and Tristan, who were like brothers to him.

"Their rejection I expected. I never fitted in at home and knew they wouldn't want anything to do with me or Theo. Your rejection hurt a lot."

"I never intended to hurt you," he said, thinking about the pain he'd carefully disguised as anger when he'd caught her in his brother's arms. The anger that he'd used to mask the vulnerability he'd felt at having trusted her.

"Of course, you didn't. Now that you know Theo's your son, is everything magically fixed in the past?"

He didn't hesitate, because the one time he had, with her, had brought them to this moment. "I had the test performed, but I haven't read the results."

"Then why have the test done?"

"I needed proof on this so that I could trust you."

"You needed *proof*? Trust doesn't work that way. Relationships are built on a belief in the other person, not facts and tests, and I can't live with a man who doesn't trust me."

"Are you threatening to leave?" he asked. He wanted to toss her over his shoulder, take her up to his room and lock her in. Ensure that she could never leave. But on the outside he struggled to play it cool.

"You sound as if it doesn't matter to you," she said.

"Hell, yes, it matters to me. But I'm not going to beg you to forgive me for something that was necessary."

She shook her head. "What do you mean necessary?"

"You wanted me to trust you, to believe in you and I wanted to give you that. To be able to love you the way you deserve…"

"And the only way you could do that was to go behind my back and have Theo tested?" she asked.

He took a step toward her, because this time she hadn't sounded defensive or angry. She'd sounded confused.

"You wanted something from me that I'm not capable of giving."

"What do you think I want from you?"

"Blind trust."

"I didn't want blind anything, Christos. I wanted love. Full-on, head-over-heels love. The kind of stuff that you read about in old epic tales."

He rubbed the back of his neck, trying to ease the tension there. "That's not realistic."

"I know what reality is and I know what I feel. And I love you that way, Christos."

Suddenly nothing else mattered. "You love me?"

She shrugged. "Yes, I do. But I can't live with you if you are going to lie to me, especially where Theo is concerned."

She walked past him and out of the room. He just stood there, thinking about her words. She loved him. What did that mean? Was that the emotion that had been buzzing around inside of him? Was that what all the possessiveness and jealousy he felt around her stemmed from?

He realized at that instant what Ava had meant by needing his trust, because there was no way he was ever going to be able to find proof of her love unless he simply believed her.

Ava felt small and very much the little girl from the trailer park as she left Christos and went out on the balcony that overlooked the vast, landscaped gardens at the Theakis compound. The house was huge and she had no idea where Theo was, but she wanted to see her son. Wanted to cuddle his little body next to hers and just bask for a few minutes in his unconditional love.

"What are you fighting with my son about?"

Surprised, she looked up at Ari as he came out onto the balcony in his wheelchair. He was the last person she'd talk about her problems with. In fact she suspected he'd probably applaud her problems with Christos and have Maria pack her bags and drive her to the airport.

"It's none of your business," she said at last.

"Everything that affects the Theakis family is my business."

"Did you meddle in Stavros and Nikki's marriage like this?" she asked. Anything to change the topic from her and Christos.

He sighed and for a moment she saw every one of Ari's eighty-one years on his face. "No. Stavros and Nikki…they had their own way of working things out. I didn't understand them."

"Me, neither," Ava said.

"You got caught in the middle of one of their games."

Ava knew that but was surprised to hear it from Ari. "What do you know about that?"

"I know everything that happens in my kingdom."

"This isn't a kingdom."

"Stop giving me a hard time. And stop letting the past dictate your future. You married Christos and are his wife—it's time you acted as if those vows meant something to you."

She glared down at him, thinking about broken vows, and knew she wasn't the one who had started this. But then again, this wasn't an elementary-school game of blame. "I take my vows very seriously, Ari, but some things…I can't compromise to make my marriage work. It's silly and probably American, but I can't change the fact that I want my husband to trust me."

Ava wrapped her arms around her waist and turned away from her father-in-law. Had her dreams of marriage been too unrealistic? Had she somehow been brainwashed by too many Disney animated films as a young girl? She'd never thought so. She'd seen evidence of happily married people.

And all of her single friends were looking for the same thing she was. They wanted the spouse and the kids and the other crazy stuff that went along with them. Not an idealized version of family life, but the reality of it. And Ava knew that had to start with trust. Because if she and Christos had a real marriage there were going to be fights, and only with real love could they weather those storms.

"You remind me a lot of my wife."

"I thought you didn't like me," she said.

"I don't. You're too stubborn and refuse to do what I say…that's exactly how Leka was. You have that same fire and passion when it comes to protecting your son and standing up to me."

"Why are you telling me this?"

"Because you look like you are finally thinking of giving up, and that's not who you really are."

"Ari, I've tried. I can't make Christos trust me, and without that everything else is built on air."

"Why do you think he doesn't trust you?"

"I asked him to believe my word that Theo was his son."

"The paternity test was legitimate. We had to have it for insurance purposes."

"The Theakis men do whatever they want. If he'd wanted to, Christos could just have said Theo was his son."

"He's not the only one who decides these things," Ari said.

"Are you saying you're the one who asked the doctor to administer the test?" she asked, knowing perfectly well that Ari hadn't. Christos had admitted to doing the deed himself, but she wondered how far Ari would go to try to convince her to stay.

"I was going to, but I can tell from your tone that you know it was Christos."

"Yes, I do." She sighed again. She felt so hollow inside and had no idea how to get back to normal.

"It's not that Christos doesn't believe in you, Ava, it's that he's afraid to believe in you."

"I don't follow."

"When my Leka died, Christos was young—only nine. He was very close to his mother, and even when he was a young child, he and I never saw eye-to-eye. And her loss was…hard on all of us, but especially on Christos."

Ava imagined how Theo would react if she were taken from his life. It was a heart-wrenching thought and made her really feel for Christos.

"What does this have to do with the man he is now?" she asked.

Ari pushed his sunglasses onto his forehead and looked her straight in the eye. "He stopped letting anyone into his life. He put up a barrier that only those two hellions he hangs out with were ever able to get past."

She wanted to smile at the way he described Guillermo and Tristan. They were two of the wealthiest and most successful men in the world, yet to Ari they were hellions.

"I still don't see what this has to do with me."

"I think he's testing you to see if you'll stay."

She shook her head. She had no doubt he was testing her in some way. But what Ari said… "I'm not sure I believe that."

"I've known him all his life, Ava, and I haven't seen him smile the way he does around you and Theo since he was a little boy.

"I've lost one son and am not going to give up on the one I have left now that he's finally found his way back."

Ava shook her head. "You can't make him love me."

"No, but you can."

"I'm not going to. I've spent my entire life striving for things out of my reach and just once I'd like someone to put me first."

"Christos already does that with you. He cuts his days in the office short to spend more time with you and Theo. Think about that." And Ari wheeled around and left her there.

Ava sighed and made her way back to her own room. She couldn't bring herself to go back to Christos's bed. Not yet.

She wished she could believe that Christos had been motivated by love, but she didn't think she could. She'd fooled herself twice into thinking that Christos loved her, and she'd been wrong.

* * *

Ava came out of the house the next afternoon and found Christos and Theo playing in the pool. She knew that Christos had been teaching Theo to swim but watching her son jump from the pool deck into the water made her breath catch. He surfaced quickly, swam to the edge and got out again.

"Mama, watch this," Theo said.

"What am I watching?"

"Cannonball!" He jumped into the pool with a big splash of water.

Christos stayed in the water but swam over near her. Resting his tanned muscled arms on the side, he looked up at her.

"How are you?" he asked, softly.

There was real concern in his voice. Or was she just imagining it? Hearing what she wanted to. "Fine."

"Ava, I don't like this distance between us."

"I didn't put it there."

"How can I make it up to you?"

"You can't, Christos. There was only one way to prove you trusted me."

"Mama?"

"Yes, Theo?"

"Watch this."

"I am watching."

She looked away from Christos to stare at Theo. But what she saw was the fact that her son used to be afraid of the water and being here with Christos had changed that. Being with Christos had changed *them*. She'd always been afraid of who she was, but Christos had given her the strength to be herself.

"Theo, enough for today. I have to go back to work."

"Ok, *Baba*."

Theo swam to the side where Christos was and hugged him. Ava lifted him out of the pool. Theo hugged her and then ran to the poolside table where Maria had placed lemonade and snacks.

Christos got out of the pool and stood next to her. It was the closest they'd been since their fight. "I can teach our son not to fear water, *moro mou*, but I don't know how to teach you to trust me. I know that you can't see past what I did, but the reasons were more complex than just your trust."

"Your father told me. Tried to take the blame for the test."

Christos shook his head. "I ordered the test, I did that. But I haven't looked at the results, and I won't."

Ava felt the first chink of doubt in her resolve that his forcing the test was a bad idea. She watched him walk away, seeing for the first time that they both had to trust each other. She had to believe in him when he made promises to her, and she hadn't.

Christos spent the next two days at the office trying to tell himself that he didn't need a close relationship with Ava to be happy. But he missed her. He wanted her back in his bed. At night when he came home to tuck

Theo in he'd prompt the boy for stories about his mother so he could find out how she was doing.

God, he was pitiful.

The love he wasn't sure he felt for her was now seeming more and more real. He ached to have her back in his bed, not just so they could make love, but also so they could talk about the day.

He knew only one person who'd been in love, who knew what real heartbreak was. And though he'd always been careful to keep his emotions private, he had nowhere else to turn. Life with Ava couldn't continue this way.

He left Theo's room and walked down the hall to his study. The room was filled with items he'd collected and had at one time been a sanctuary for him, but no longer. Now it just seemed so much emptier than it ever had before.

He dialed Tristan's number before he could change his mind and without calculating the time difference from Mykonos to Manhattan.

"Theakis, it's the middle of the day here."

"I'm sorry, this couldn't wait."

"What's the matter? Is it Theo or Ava?"

"It's…ah, hell, Tristan, I've screwed things up with Ava. You said something on our wedding day about women's dreams…and I've never really understood what she wants from me."

"Ask her."

"What?"

"Ask her. She'll tell you what her dreams are and then you can fulfill them."

He knew what Ava wanted and realized he'd backed himself into a corner. "She wants me to love her and trust her."

"You don't really trust anyone," Tristan said.

"I trust you and Gui."

"Now, you do. But you didn't for the first fifteen years we knew each other."

"I don't think Ava's going to give me that much time."

"Having met her, I'd agree. What's the hold-up here? Is it the relationship with Stavros?"

No, it wasn't. It was him and the damned hollowness inside that he knew was the wellspring of his aloofness. That distance he kept as a buffer between him and the world.

"No, that's not it."

"What is it then?"

He couldn't put it into words with Tristan. "Nothing."

"It sounds like you love her, *mon ami*. Don't let her slip away. She's the first good thing to happen to you since…well, ever. She's the kind of woman who can give you the home and family you've always wanted."

"I wasn't looking for home and family."

"Whatever you say."

He wished it really was whatever he said. Because then he'd order Ava to move back to his room and make their lives together everything she wanted them to be. "Later."

He hung up the phone as everything coalesced in his

head. He needed Ava even more than he needed Theo or Ari or the Theakis shipping business. He needed her because she made him feel alive. Before her, he'd been stuck in the rut that came from always running and never standing still.

Did he love her?

Yes, he thought. He did love her. She was the only woman who'd ever made an impression on him. The only woman who'd ever made him feel so many different things. The only woman he'd never been able to forget.

He needed to find Ava and tell her that he loved her. Tell her that he'd been an idiot for not believing in her. Because now he understood what she wanted from him.

He went to the bedroom she'd moved back into two days ago and knocked on the door.

The door opened and she stood there in her bare feet and bathrobe. Her face was scrubbed clean of makeup and her hair was pulled back. His breath caught in his throat as the love he felt for her swamped him.

She kept the door partially closed like a barrier between them and he realized he wasn't going to let her do this. Let her turn him into some kind of simpering fool because he loved her.

He pushed the door open and scooped her up in his arms. He kicked the door closed and carried her across the room. He tossed her down on the center of the bed and then covered her body with his own.

She wedged her hands between them pushing against his chest. "What are you doing?"

"Claiming my wife."

"You already did that on our wedding night."

"No I didn't," he said, bending down to kiss her because the words hovering on the tip of his tongue were too revealing.

He plundered her mouth and restaked his claim on her. Tried to show her with his body all the things that he struggled to find the words to say. Her hands skimmed over his chest up to his neck, wrapping around his shoulders.

"I've missed you, *moro mou*."

"I've missed you, too. But sex isn't going to make everything okay between us," she said. "I want more than this from you."

"What do you want, Ava?"

"You to know that I trust you. So I have something for you."

"What?"

"Go sit down and I'll show you."

"Show me?"

"Yes."

She got up and walked away from Christos and he watched her go. She returned with an envelope, handing it to him. "I had this done because I don't want to test you or your love. I need to trust you as well."

"What is it?"

"Another paternity test. Open it and put your doubts to rest. I know that the situation you found me in with Stavros and the lies that I'd told you about my background all contributed to what you believed of me."

"Ava, I trust you. I know—"

She put her fingers over his lips. "Just let me do this for us."

He pulled her down on his lap and she snuggled close to him as he opened the envelope and pulled out the paper inside. He didn't look at it but instead stared down at her. "This can't change the way I feel about you. I trust you with my entire heart."

"That's wonderful, Christos, but I want more."

Thirteen

"I want more, too," Christos said. "I want your love."

A tear trailed down her cheek. "I haven't stopped loving you."

"Good."

She smiled, thinking of the test results that waited on that paper. She wasn't sure what he'd say, but it was the only olive branch she had. "Good?" He still hadn't looked at it.

"I think I meant fantastic."

"Why?"

"Because I love you, too. I think I always did. But I've been afraid to let you see how much you matter to me."

"Oh, Christos, why?"

"Because…" Christos whispered in her ear. "If I didn't love you, then it wouldn't matter if you left me."

"I'm not going anywhere."

"I know," he said, shifting her more comfortably in his lap.

"Your father was sure you were testing me."

"I think I was testing myself. Can you forgive me for not believing in you?"

"Yes. I can."

He took her mouth with his, letting his hands wander over her body. He untied the sash at her waist and pushed the sides of her robe open. She shivered and undulated against him. He leaned down to lick each nipple until it tightened. Then he blew gently on the tips. She raked her nails down his back.

"Oh, Christos, I'm afraid to believe this is real."

"Doesn't it feel real?" He shifted to lay her on the bed then moved further down her body, kissing his way over her stomach, his tongue tracing over the silvery stretch marks and lingering on her belly button.

He continued moving lower until he hovered right over her center.

"Open yourself for me," he said.

Her legs moved, but he took her hands in his, bringing them to her mound. She hesitated but then did as he asked.

"Hold still," he said.

He leaned down, blowing lightly on her before drawing her flesh into his mouth. He skimmed his hands up her thighs, then lifted his head and looked up her body.

Her eyes were closed, her head tipped back, her shoulders arched, throwing her breasts out.

He lowered his head again, hungry for more of her. He feasted on her body the way a starving man would, giving her as much pleasure as he could to celebrate the joy she brought to his life.

He wanted this night when they'd both confessed their love to each other to be one she never forgot. He concentrated on driving her toward her climax. He used his teeth, tongue and fingers to bring her to the brink but held her there, wanting to draw out the moment of completion until she was begging him for it.

Her hands left her body, grasping his head as she thrust her hips up toward his face. But he pulled back so that she didn't get the contact she craved.

"Christos, now."

He scraped his teeth over her and she cried out as her orgasm rocked through her body. He kept his mouth on her until her body stopped shuddering and then slid up her.

"Your turn," she said, pushing him over onto his back.

She took his erection in her hand then followed with her tongue, teasing him with quick licks and light touches. But he was too close to the edge to let her continue. He pulled her away from his body, wanting to be inside her.

He moved her until she straddled his hips. Then, carefully, he pulled her down while he pushed into her body.

He pulled her legs forward, moving them farther apart until she settled even closer to him.

He slid deeper still into her. She arched her back, reaching up to entwine her arms around his shoulders. He thrust harder and felt every nerve in his body tensing. Reaching between their bodies he touched her between her legs until he felt her body start to tighten around him.

This time they cried out together, and then she collapsed on top of him, her head on his chest.

As they lay snuggled together, he found peace and contentment with her. Something he'd never known he'd want or need.

There was one more thing he had to do. He reached for the paper with the paternity test results, which had ended up next to Ava on the bed. Slowly, without looking at it, he tore it into tiny pieces and let them flutter out of his fingers. "Now, do you believe I love you?"

"Yes," she said.

* * * * *

Christos may have finally been tamed,
but Tristan Sabina's story is just beginning.
Don't miss the next sexy and exciting
SONS OF PRIVILEGE *story*
from Katherine Garbera,
THE WEALTHY FRENCHMAN'S PROPOSITION

On sale in February 2008.
Only from Silhouette Desire!

Silhouette® Desire

NEW YORK TIMES BESTSELLING AUTHOR

DIANA PALMER

A brand-new Long, Tall Texans novel

IRON COWBOY

*Available March 2008
wherever you buy books.*

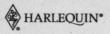

Silhouette®

Romantic
SUSPENSE

**Sparked by Danger,
Fueled by Passion.**

When Tech Sergeant Jacob "Mako" Stone opens
his door to a mysterious woman without a past,
he knows his time off is over. As threats to Dee's
life bring her and Jacob together, she must set
aside her pride and accept the help of the military
hero with too many secrets of his own.

Out of Uniform
by Catherine Mann

Available February wherever you buy books.

HARLEQUIN® *Super Romance*®

Texas Hold 'Em

When it comes to love, the stakes are high

Sixteen years ago, Luke Chisum dated
Becky Parker on a dare…before going
on to break her heart. Now the former
River Bluff daredevil is back, rekindling
desire and tempting Becky to pick up
where they left off. But this time she has
to resist or Luke could discover the secret
she's kept locked away all these years.…

Look for

TEXAS BLUFF

by *Linda Warren*
#1470

Available February 2008
wherever you buy books.

$1.00 OFF

The bestselling Lakeshore Chronicles continue with *Snowfall at Willow Lake*, a story of what comes after a woman survives an unspeakable horror and finds her way home, to healing and redemption and a new chance at happiness.

SUSAN WIGGS

NEW YORK TIMES BESTSELLING AUTHOR

SUSAN WIGGS

"Susan Wiggs's novels are beautiful, tender and wise."
—Luanne Rice

Snowfall at Willow Lake
The Lakeshore Chronicles

On sale February 2008!

SAVE $1.00 off the purchase price of **SNOWFALL AT WILLOW LAKE** by **Susan Wiggs.**

Offer valid from February 1, 2008, to April 30, 2008.
Redeemable at participating retail outlets. Limit one coupon per purchase.

5 2 6 0 8 1 6 8

5 65373 00076 2 (8100) 0 11463

MSW2493CPN

REQUEST YOUR FREE BOOKS!

2 FREE NOVELS PLUS 2 FREE GIFTS!

Passionate, Powerful, Provocative!

YES! Please send me 2 FREE Silhouette Desire® novels and my 2 FREE gifts. After receiving them, if I don't wish to receive any more books, I can return the shipping statement marked "cancel." If I don't cancel, I will receive 6 brand-new novels every month and be billed just $3.80 per book in the U.S., or $4.47 per book in Canada, plus 25¢ shipping and handling per book and applicable taxes, if any*. That's a savings of almost 15% off the cover price! I understand that accepting the 2 free books and gifts places me under no obligation to buy anything. I can always return a shipment and cancel at any time. Even if I never buy another book from Silhouette, the two free books and gifts are mine to keep forever.

225 SDN EEXJ 326 SDN EEXU

Name	(PLEASE PRINT)	
Address		Apt.
City	State/Prov.	Zip/Postal Code

Signature (if under 18, a parent or guardian must sign)

Mail to the **Silhouette Reader Service™:**
IN U.S.A.: P.O. Box 1867, Buffalo, NY 14240-1867
IN CANADA: P.O. Box 609, Fort Erie, Ontario L2A 5X3

Not valid to current Silhouette Desire subscribers.

Want to try two free books from another line?
Call 1-800-873-8635 or visit www.morefreebooks.com.

* Terms and prices subject to change without notice. NY residents add applicable sales tax. Canadian residents will be charged applicable provincial taxes and GST. This offer is limited to one order per household. All orders subject to approval. Credit or debit balances in a customer's account(s) may be offset by any other outstanding balance owed by or to the customer. Please allow 4 to 6 weeks for delivery.

Your Privacy: Silhouette is committed to protecting your privacy. Our Privacy Policy is available online at www.eHarlequin.com or upon request from the Reader Service. From time to time we make our lists of customers available to reputable firms who may have a product or service of interest to you. If you would prefer we not share your name and address, please check here. ☐

SDES07

You can lead a horse to water...

When Alyssa Barkley and Clint Westmoreland
found out that their "fake" marriage was never
rendered void, they are forced to live together
for thirty days. However, Clint loves the single
life and has no intention of being tamed, but
when Alyssa moves in, the sizzling attraction
between them is ignited and neither wants the
thirty days to end.

Look for

TAMING CLINT
WESTMORELAND

by

BRENDA
JACKSON

Available February wherever you buy books

COMING NEXT MONTH

#1849 PRIDE & A PREGNANCY SECRET—
Tessa Radley

Diamonds Down Under

She wants to be more than his secret mistress, especially now that she's pregnant with his heir. But she isn't the only one with a secret that could shatter a legacy.

#1850 TAMING CLINT WESTMORELAND—
Brenda Jackson

They thought their fake marriage was over...until they discovered they were still legally bound—with their attraction as strong as ever.

#1851 THE WEALTHY FRENCHMAN'S PROPOSITION—
Katherine Garbera

Sons of Privilege

Sleeping with her billionaire boss was not on her agenda. But discovering they were suddenly engaged was an even bigger surprise!

#1852 DANTE'S BLACKMAILED BRIDE—Day Leclaire
The Dante Legacy

He had to have her. And once he discovered her secret, he had the perfect opportunity to blackmail his business rival's daughter into becoming his bride.

#1853 BEAUTY AND THE BILLIONAIRE—
Barbara Dunlop

A business mogul must help his newest employee transform from plain Jane to Cinderella princess...but can he keep his hands off her once his job's done?

#1854 TYCOON'S VALENTINE VENDETTA—
Yvonne Lindsay

Rekindling a forbidden romance with the daughter of his sworn enemy was the perfect way to get his revenge. Then he discovers she's pregnant with his child!

SDCNM0108